# Torrie & the Firebird

Text by
## K.V. Johansen

Illustrations by
## Christine Delezenne

**annick press**
toronto + new york + vancouver

Text © 2006 K.V. Johansen
Illustrations © 2006 Christine Delezenne
Map © 2006 K.V. Johansen

**Annick Press Ltd.**

We acknowledge the support of the Canada Council for the Arts, the Ontario Arts Council, and the Government of Canada through the Book Publishing Industry Development Program (BPIDP) for our publishing activities.

Edited by Pam Robertson
Copy edited by Elizabeth McLean
Proofread by Derek Fairbridge
Cover and interior design by Irvin Cheung/iCheung Design
Cover and interior illustrations by Christine Delezenne

The text was typeset in Perpetua and Egyptienne

**Cataloging in Publication**
Johansen, K.V. (Krista V.), 1968–
     Torrie and the firebird / text by K.V. Johansen ; illustrations by
Christine Delezenne.

(The Torrie quests)
ISBN-13: 978-1-55037-961-7 (bound)
ISBN-10: 1-55037-961-5 (bound)
ISBN-13: 978-1-55037-960-0 (pbk.)
ISBN-10: 1-55037-960-7 (pbk.)

     I. Delezenne, Christine  II. Title.  III. Series.
PS8569.O2676T674 2006     jC813'.54     C2005-906856-6

| Published in the U.S.A. by | Distributed in Canada by | Distributed in the U.S.A. by |
|---|---|---|
| Annick Press (U.S.) Ltd. | Firefly Books Ltd. | Firefly Books (U.S.) Inc. |
| | 66 Leek Crescent | P.O. Box 1338 |
| | Richmond Hill, ON | Ellicott Station |
| | L4B 1H1 | Buffalo, NY 14205 |

Printed and bound in Canada
Visit our website at **www.annickpress.com**

This one is for my nephew and godson Julian, with many thanks to Allen Keast, honorary uncle

# Glossary of People, Places, Things, and Old Things

## People

**Anna:** captain of the *Shrike*, which isn't a pirate ship anymore, although Anna's crew is sometimes a little disappointed about that.

**Annapurna Khanum** (AN-na-PUR-na KAH-num): an explorer who writes books about exotic places; Kokako's favorite author. Annapurna comes from a *very* interesting family ...

**Banksy:** a retired pirate, ship's carpenter on the *Shrike*; he's married to Galeata.

**Lord Barramundi** (BAR-ra-MUN-di): a sorcerer who thinks things would be better if he were in charge. Lots of people think that; they're usually wrong.

**Delena** (De-LEH-na): the girl who sweeps the spiders out of the *Oyon*-Shrine.

**Frederik:** crown prince of the Granite Isles. In an earlier adventure, Anna and Torrie rescued him, made his mother, the pirate-queen, give up piracy, and lifted the curse on the Granite Isles. He's not in this story, but Anna thinks he's important.

**Galeata** (GAL-eh-a-ta): a retired pirate, another carpenter on the *Shrike;* she's married to Banksy.

**Icterus** (IC-tair-us): Anna's father, a sea captain.

**Jabiru** (Ja-BEE-ru): a magistrate from Keastipol, who is also chief magistrate of the Parliament of Seventy.

**Jix:** Kokako's parrot (he's a western king parrot, also called a red-capped parrot).

**Kokako** (Ko-KA-ko): a floor-sweeper in the *Oyon*-Shrine who's accused of destroying the *Oyon*-Shrine.

**Mirimick** (MEER-ee-mick): a retired pirate, bow master on the *Shrike*.

**Mister Flytch:** Anna's first mate on the *Shrike* (and, of course, a retired pirate). Sometimes Anna isn't sure how retired he really wants to be.

**Tero Korax the Wanderer** (TER-o KOR-ax): a legendary person. She gave the cities of the Great Southern Continent the *Oyon* as a symbol of peace and set up the Parliament of Seventy, a hundred years before this story begins.

## Places

**Arcaringa Salt Lake** (ARK-a-RING-gah): a salt lake out between the Gunyidy and Dandarigan deserts. Not a good place to go fishing.

**Bookabee Highlands** (BOO-ka-bee): the dry hills west of the mountains.

**Callipepla** (CAL-lee-PEPP-la): a hot country where spices come from, ruled by a sultan.

**Dandarigan Desert** (Dan-DAR-i-gan): a desert with lots of red sand, dried-up rivers, prickly grass, and scrubby bushes. Kokako thinks the deserts are beautiful, mysterious, and interesting; most people think the deserts are places to get out of as quickly as possible.

**Erythroth** (AIR-ee-throth): a northern kingdom, where Anna is originally from.

**Fengu Forest** (FEN-gu): a forest east of the mountains.

**Granite Isles:** Prince Frederik's mother's kingdom, somewhere in the South Seas northeast of the Great Southern Continent.

**Great Southern Continent:** a vast island continent in the southern hemisphere, with forests, mountains, lots of deserts, and seventy city-states, which used to fight one another all the time, but haven't since Tero Korax the Wanderer gave them the *Oyon*.

**Gunyidy Desert** (Gun-YI-dee): another desert quite a lot like the Dandarigan, except even hotter.

**Keastipol** (KEAST-i-pol): the biggest of the city-states (a city-state is independent, like a country of its own) on the Great Southern Continent. It's where the Parliament of Seventy meets.

**Mundaring Mountains** (Mun-DAR-ing): a mountain range on the eastern side of the Great Southern Continent. Not a hugely high mountain range like the mountains near the Wild Forest (or the Alps or the Himalayas), but quite high enough if you have to climb over them.

**Whenualand** (Whe-NOO-a-land): a kingdom of two islands, east of the Great Southern Continent. Where Kokako's father was from.

**Wild Forest:** a great forest in the northern part of the world, separated from Erythroth by very high mountains. Torrie says he is the oldest Old Thing of the Wild Forest.

## Things

**Oyon** (OY-on): a big oval piece of opal. (Opals are gemstones: they're usually milky white with shimmery rainbow colors in them.) The most precious thing to all the people of the Great

Southern Continent. Its proper name is the *Oyon-Opallion* (OY-on-o-PAL-lee-on), but nobody calls it that anymore except in old history books.

**The *Oyon*-Shrine:** a white marble building with lots of pillars, on a hill overlooking the city of Keastipol. Like a cross between a temple and a museum; it's where the *Oyon* is kept, and where Kokako works as a sweeper.

**Parliament of Seventy:** Each city-state of the Great Southern Continent sends one magistrate to the Parliament, so that arguments can be settled between the cities without going to war. The Parliament elects a chief magistrate to run the meetings. (A magistrate is like a judge, and, on the Great Southern Continent, a politician, too.)

*Shrike:* Anna's ship. The *Shrike* is a type of medieval ship called a cog.

### Old Things

*Old Things are ancient, magical beings; in the time that this story takes place, many humans don't believe in them anymore. That's alright. Many Old Things would rather not believe in humans, either. Some Old Things say they have been in the world as long as humans have, or longer ... but they like to tell stories, so who knows? There are many different kinds of Old Things. Some are interesting to meet; some you should probably run away from, very, very quickly. Many Old Things cannot be seen by humans unless the Old Thing actually wants to be seen. Others, like goblins, can't hide from humans this way, but are very good at being sneaky. Some look a lot like humans; most don't. Although some of them have magical powers, Old Things don't usually do flashy magic; they leave that kind of thing for human sorcerers. Old Things are magic. They're always most powerful when they're in their own place, that is, the place they belong to, the way Torrie belongs to the Wild Forest.*

**Dingobreath, Stonefang,** and **Seventoes:** sand-goblins (*see below*).

**Fair Folk:** You might call them fairies, but only if you were *really* foolish, since these days, people usually assume fairies are the tiny, delicate creatures with butterfly wings. (Once upon a time, all Old Things were called fairies by humans—then it was just those who looked human-shaped, and in Torrie's world by the time that this story happens, it's only the tiny ones. There's nothing wrong with being four inches tall with butterfly wings, but if you're dealing with a very proud and short-tempered six-and-a-half-foot-tall warrior ... well, it's not a good idea to get mixed up about which is which, that's all.) The Fair Folk look like tall, handsome humans, more or less. There was once a Fair Folk man who married a human princess of Callipepla, and they had two children, hundreds of years before this story begins. Their children were more or less human, but they were as long-lived as Old Things. Their daughter became a wandering minstrel and their son, who had never fit in at court in Callipepla, grew up to be a sorcerer ...

**The Firebird:** a legendary bird of fire, with an amazing song. Even other Old Things think the Firebird is just a myth.

**Rock-folk:** creatures of living rock, found mostly in the Great Southern Continent. They're big, hot like molten lava, with a crust of hardening stone, and speak very slowly, which doesn't mean they're stupid.

**Sand-goblins:** closely related to the hairy, gray goblins of the Wild Forest and the northern mountains, but are the color of the red sand of the deserts of the Great Southern Continent. Like ordinary goblins, they like to live underground in big groups. They're quarrelsome, like to smash and destroy things, and will eat anything. They're also not too bright.

**Torrie:** oldest of the Old Things of the Wild Forest, which is very far away from where this story takes place. He likes to go on adventures with young humans, to see what sort of interesting things will happen to them.

**Wind Dancers:** Old Things of the air, who live mostly over the deserts of the Great Southern Continent. They don't have bodies that humans can see or feel, but are more like spirits.

To Granite Isles

Paraburdupol

Gunyidy Desert

Arcaringa
Salt Lake

Mundiwindipol

Fengu
Forest

Bookabee
Highlands

Dandarigan
Desert

Mooloogoolipol

Sleeping River

Mundaring Mts.

KEASTIPOL

N

W          E

Great Southern
Continent (East Coast)

S

Irribiddipol

# CHAPTER ONE

# In which Kokako meets some goblins

If you recall, I promised to tell you the story of the adventure I had on the Great Southern Continent, when I sailed there with Anna. Although she was quite young, as humans go, Anna was a master mariner, captain of the *Shrike*, which used to be a pirate ship but wasn't anymore. Anna didn't expect anything very exciting to happen on that voyage. She was going to sell the salt fish she had in her hold from the retired pirates' last fishing expedition, and buy trees for our friend Prince Frederik of the Granite Isles, so that he could plant new forests on his barren kingdom. Simple. But, you're probably thinking, not very exciting.

I thought so, too. I was still in a mood for adventure when we sailed to the Great Southern Continent, and luckily, I still had that itchy, fidgety feeling in my feet, which told me something interesting was about to happen.

Almost as soon as we tied up at a wharf in the great, bustling harbor of the city of Keastipol, something interesting did happen. Anna and I weren't there for the start of it all, though we came into it later. In the very beginning, there was just a boy named Kokako, waking up in the night with a strange sound ringing in his ears.

≈≈≈≈≈

Kokako lay very still, straining to hear. The sound was gone, now. There was nothing disturbing the night but his own breathing. For a moment, though, he was sure he had heard something, a sound that was both very large, and very quiet, like a giant's sigh. He must have heard something, he told himself, or he wouldn't have woken up. And since he was the only person who slept in the building called the *Oyon*-Shrine, which was a bit like a shrine or holy place and a bit like a museum, high on a hill overlooking the city of Keastipol, it was up to him to investigate.

Carefully, Kokako felt around until he found his tunic and his sandals. If there were someone out in the main hall, a thief or even just a stray dingo dog, he didn't want to run into anyone wearing only his drawers. It's hard to feel brave and bold wearing nothing but your underwear.

Kokako's bed was a cot in one of the little back storerooms of the *Oyon*-Shrine, but he didn't mind. During the day, the *Oyon*-Shrine was filled with visitors who came from all the cities of the Great Southern Continent, but at night, when the other servants went home to their houses in the city, it became his own private palace. Nobody else could say that.

The *Oyon*-Shrine truly was one of the most beautiful buildings in the whole world. You reached it by climbing uphill on a broad flight of stairs and then entering a porch of many pillars, all in white marble. If you looked up before you went in, you saw carved scenes from history—scenes of warriors fighting and towers burning, as the seventy cities of the Great Southern Continent fought one another in their terrible wars, which usually started over some fairly pointless argument. In the past, there had been wars about whether the sky was blue or azure (which means "sky blue"), wars about whose mountains were higher, wars about which city was the first to make some important discovery or was the best at some art or grew the best grapes or raised the best sheep. Then, in the carvings, you'd see the appearance of the woman they called Tero Korax the Wanderer, a foreign minstrel always shown with a harp slung over her shoulder and two feathers stuck in her hair. She was the one who had formed the first Parliament of Seventy, to which each city had sent one magistrate—a magistrate is a person rather like a judge. The Parliament was supposed to settle arguments between the cities without war.

Most importantly, there were carvings showing Tero Korax the Wanderer giving the Seventy Magistrates the *Oyon*. This was a large gemstone, an opal so big even a grown man would need both hands to carry it, milky white and shimmering with streaks and flecks of orange and scarlet and green. In old poetry and history books it was actually called the *Oyon-*

*Opallion*. Kokako liked the sound of the old words, rich and thick like honey in your mouth, mysterious and opal-y, but nobody used the proper name anymore, not even the oldest of the magistrates. The *Oyon* didn't do anything. It just sat on an altar in the *Oyon*-Shrine, a symbol of the peace between the cities that had by then lasted for a hundred years. People believed that so long as the *Oyon* was safe in the *Oyon*-Shrine, the Great Southern Continent would go on having peace. It wasn't that easy, of course. Many times they came to the brink of war. Magistrates shouted and screamed and punched one another in the Parliament, and stormed off home vowing never to come back. But they always did, and war never quite happened, because everybody knew that the *Oyon* stood for peace. It reminded them to try a bit harder.

Inside, the main hall of the *Oyon*-Shrine was a vast, cool, dimly pale space, with white marble floors, marble walls, more marble pillars, and even a marble roof. Thin sheets of translucent stone let in a bright glow by day, and at night the moon washed it in the faintest misty light. In the center of this echoing space was the altar (marble, of course). It was decorated with scented branches cut from groves of different kinds of eucalypt or gum trees that grew around the *Oyon*-Shrine. On the altar was the *Oyon* itself.

In the evenings, when all the visitors had gone, Kokako would sometimes sit with his back against the altar, reading the books of travel and adventure he borrowed from the library. He read the best bits, especially by his favorite author, the explorer Annapurna Khanum, out loud to Jix, his parrot, who sat on his shoulder making hoarse chuckling noises from time to time. He always felt as though the *Oyon* were listening, too. The big oval opal had always seemed, to Kokako, like something alive.

But that was only when there was no one around. During the busy day he was just the sweeper, the lowest of all the servants. It was his job to sweep the polished marble floor, chasing out all the dust that the dozens, even hundreds, of visitors tracked in every day. Even Delena, the pretty girl who dusted the corners for spiders, thought she was better than Kokako.

Someday, though, Kokako was going to do more. He would be a scientist and go off on long journeys of exploration and teach at the academy, as his mother had done. He could hardly remember those long-ago days. She and his father, a sailor from the eastern island kingdom of Whenualand, had been lost at sea in a typhoon, leaving Kokako and his grandmother all alone in Keastipol. After his grandmother died, there was no one to look after him at all. He knew he was really very lucky to have a job as a sweeper, but there was no way he was going to stay a sweeper all his life. Although capturing a burglar wasn't science, it would be a good start to a life of adventure.

In case the noise actually was a burglar, or worse, burglars, Kokako woke up Jix, too. It's also a lot easier to be brave when you have company. Jix grumbled and kept his eyes shut, but he dug his claws into Kokako's shoulder and hung on.

Without even the faintest glimmer of moonlight to see by, Kokako crept along a low-ceilinged, windowless passage and edged out into the main hall of the *Oyon*-Shrine. There, he could see, once his eyes adjusted. The vast space was lit by pearly moonlight coming through the thin, cloudy stone of the roof. The pillars loomed out of the thick shadows like a forest of white-barked ghost-gum trees. Kokako could see several dark shapes standing between him and the altar, where there shouldn't be any dark shapes at all. Behind the shapes, he could just make out the dim sheen of the *Oyon*, like a second moon.

Then one of the dark shapes moved, turning its head to look directly at Kokako. It had red, glowing eyes.

Jix, who was peeking with his eyes half-open, gave a startled squawk and flew off into the shadows. Kokako stopped breathing.

The eyes continued to glare scarlet and orange, like liquid bronze being poured into a mold, or iron when the blacksmith first takes it out of the fire and begins hammering it. Then the light winked out as the shadowy shape turned away, leaving funny greenish white splotches dancing in Kokako's vision. He took a deep, careful breath. Whatever it was, it hadn't actually seen him. Or it didn't think he was important enough to bother with.

"They've made it so easy," said a man's voice. And then Kokako heard a sound that made his heart give a sort of lurch. It was the sharp rap of someone striking flint and steel together, to make a spark. Anywhere else in the *Oyon*-Shrine it wouldn't matter, since it was all built of stone, but the altar was covered with leafy branches. It was the job of the chief magistrate to cut fresh ones, every morning. But Chief Magistrate Jabiru often didn't bother; he'd leave them until the leathery leaves were dry and crackly. And the thing about gum trees is that they're

very, very full of oil and sticky resin—that's why they're called "gum" trees, after all. So the leaves burn very, very well, once they're dry.

You can imagine what happened next.

"Don't!" Kokako shouted, but it was too late. Sparks spattered onto the twig-covered altar. He started to run towards it, thinking he could grab the *Oyon* before the fire damaged it, but a creature from a nightmare jumped up shrieking in front of him, snapping at him with sharp teeth and snatching with long-clawed fingers. Kokako stared at a crooked, pointy, sandy-red face, a long thin nose, enormous foxy ears, and a head of tufty orange hair. Its breath was worse than the worst fishy dog-breath you can imagine. He shouted and swung a fist at it, but it dodged aside with a cackle of laughter and kicked his feet out from under him.

Then there were three of them, whatever they were, and they flung themselves onto Kokako, shrieking with laughter, and sat on his back and his shoulders and his legs so he couldn't move, pinching and poking him.

"Be quiet, you lot," said the man, in a breathless, excited voice. "Be ready."

Ready for what? Kokako wondered. He squirmed, but he couldn't free himself from the creatures. The one sitting on his shoulders twisted his hair.

"Quiet," it said, in a voice like a rusty hinge. "Lord Barramundi's doing magic."

"Shh, shh, shh," hissed the others, and Kokako could feel them all staring, like people watching a magic show on the street.

The dry leaves snapped and crackled, and the scent of burning gum trees filled the air. It was spicy and sharp, but at the same time harsh and choking, and the oily smoke crawled around the great hall. Kokako coughed, and the creatures holding him coughed, but then they all shouted at once, the way people do when they're watching fireworks. A great pillar of flame roared up from the altar, and when it hit the roof it spread out so it looked like a giant tree rising over them.

There was a terrible cracking noise, and pieces of the roof began to crumble and fall in small fragments like hail. Ashes sifted over Kokako's upturned face. Marble really does burn, you know, if the fire is hot enough. The pillar of fire seemed to knot together, growing darker, crimson and indigo-blue and hot bronze.

"Now! Now! Now!" roared the man, waving his arms in the air.

The other big dark shape, the one that had looked at Kokako with burning eyes, moved suddenly, flinging out something like a black curtain, which whirled and fell over the pillar of fire and put it out, like smothering flames with a wet blanket. That second figure, which was either a tall fat man, or something else entirely, gathered up the blanket, or curtain, or whatever it was. It was so black that even the moonlight, bright and clear now through the hole in the roof, seemed to be swallowed up by it. And Kokako felt a cold draft blowing over him, as though the blanket were sucking up the heat.

"Is it still hot?" the man demanded impatiently.

"No, master," said the creature, and its voice was so deep

and rumbling Kokako could hardly understand it. It was more as if he felt the voice vibrating in his ribs than heard it with his ears.

"Then give it to me. And I'm not carrying you home, you're too heavy. Including you in the spell makes me too tired. Come back to the salt lake on your own and wait until I need you again."

"Yes, master."

The man took the black bundle. The thing with the glowing eyes—Kokako was beginning to think he knew what it was, but that just shouldn't be possible, because rock-folk were for fairy tales, not real life—began to move away. It didn't exactly run, and it didn't exactly flow, but something in between, and it moved faster than a man could run, fast as a horse, or faster. It left a black, burnt mark on the floor.

"What about the boy, Lord Barramundi?" asked one of the creatures sitting on Kokako. It gave him a sharp pinch. "Can we eat him?"

The man gave a sigh, as if he couldn't be bothered with them. "Yes, fine, Stonefang, alright, eat him, if you really must."

"He's not very fat," said one of the others, prodding Kokako in the ribs with a finger.

"Scrawny, actually," said the third.

Kokako yelled and kicked, and managed to knock one of the creatures off him. It howled and grabbed his arm instead.

"Oh, for goodness' sake," said the man. "Stop playing with your food. I'm going. You'll have to get back to the salt lake on your own, too. *Try* not to get lost."

And he disappeared. *Whumph.* It was the same noise that had woken Kokako up. He didn't have time to be astonished.

"Supper, supper, supper!" sang one of the things, in a squeaky voice. "Sup-sup-suppertime!"

Kokako roared and punched that one in the nose. It burst into tears and scrambled away. The other two let go and ran to comfort it.

"Yi-yi-yi!" it wailed. "Don't do that, you big human bully!"

"I don't want to be eaten!" Kokako yelled. He rolled to his feet and stood ready to punch them again, if they came close. *Goblins.* They were sand-goblins that lived in tunnels and dens out beneath the deserts. Most city people didn't even believe they were real. He didn't *want* to believe they were real.

"Lord Barramundi didn't give us any supper," muttered one of the goblins, the one with hair all standing up in dust-stiffened spikes. "He was mad 'cause we were late getting here."

"We got lost. It was your fault, Stonefang."

"Was not!"

"It wasn't so bad, there was a henhouse," said the goblin with the bloody nose who still had speckled feathers stuck in his hair. Her hair? Kokako couldn't tell. They were all dressed in tattered skirts.

"Shut up about the henhouse, Dingobreath," said the spiky-haired one, who was Stonefang.

"You can't be very hungry at all, if you ate a whole flock of hens," said Kokako, desperately trying to remember everything he'd ever heard about sand-goblins. They weren't very clever, they weren't very brave, and they were always hungry.

"It wasn't a whole flock of hens. Stonefang let some of them get away," Dingobreath said sulkily.

"Did not!"

"Well, I'm sure there are lots of henhouses out in the hills," said Kokako. "And the hens are probably fatter than me, so why don't you go eat them?" It was hard on the farmers and their hens, of course, but that was better than *him* getting eaten.

"Tired of tough old hen. I want something tastier."

"Do you know who I am?" asked Kokako. "I'm the guardian of the *Oyon*, the demon of the *Oyon*-Shrine, and if you don't leave, I'll get angry and use my magic and put a terrible curse on you." It sounded like a fairy tale kind of thing and maybe the goblins would believe it. Just as long as they didn't think to ask why he hadn't saved the *Oyon*, if he was its guardian.

They didn't. The sand-goblins shifted from foot to foot and muttered among themselves.

"Lord Barramundi didn't say there was any demon here."

"Well, he wouldn't, would he?"

"He took off pretty quickly, and left us behind."

"He doesn't care if we get eaten by a demon."

"He doesn't love us anymore, now he's got the——"

"Shh! Shh!"

"I mean it," said Kokako, and he raised his arms as if he were about to cast a spell. He meant to run screaming at them, hoping they'd scatter so he could make it out the door and down the long flight of stairs into the city, where he could find help. As he took a deep breath, though, there was a shrieking sound from up in the darkness. Something came hurtling down from the roof. It glittered white in the moonlight and the shrill screeching was enough to make your hair stand on end.

"A ghost!"

Kokako flung himself flat on the floor and the sand-goblins fled, shoving and elbowing one another in their haste to be the first out of the *Oyon*-Shrine. The swooping, glittering white ghost, which was only about the size of a crow, followed them. They tumbled out into the night, and the sounds of their yelping died away.

Kokako climbed to his feet again and dusted the ashes of burnt marble out of his hair. He walked slowly to the altar. It

was cracked and broken. There was not a trace of the *Oyon* left, not a single broken chip of opal to show it had ever existed.

Pretty soon the ghost darted back through the door and swooped to Kokako's shoulder. Jix the parrot ruffled up his feathers and shook off a cloud of pale ash and stone dust. Then he started to preen, cleaning his feathers with his bill and making smug little croaking noises.

Kokako scratched the parrot's head.

"Good boy, Jix," he said, in a voice that had gone hoarse from all the smoke and shouting. "But now what do I do?"

Jix chattered some more and nipped his ear.

"Right," Kokako said. "I guess now we wait for Chief Magistrate Jabiru to show up."

Kokako certainly wasn't going to get to sleep again that night, so he sat down with his back against one of the pillars, hugging his knees and waiting for morning. Jix climbed on top of his head and fell asleep there, standing on one foot with the other tucked up into his feathers.

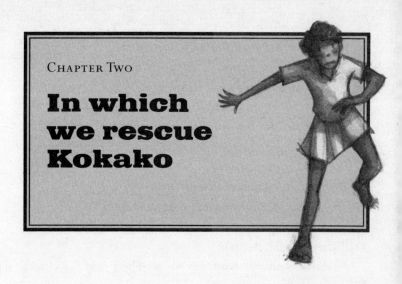

# CHAPTER TWO

# In which we rescue Kokako

It turned out that waiting for Chief Magistrate Jabiru was a big mistake.

The first person to show up in the morning was the spider-dusting girl, Delena. She took one look in through the big front doors at all the wreck and ruin, screamed, and ran away.

Delena must have run down into the city and shouted it out for everyone to hear: the *Oyon* had been burned up in a fire. By the time Chief Magistrate Jabiru and most of the sixty-nine other magistrates showed up, there was already a big crowd in the *Oyon*-Shrine. The commander of the city watch was making Kokako tell his story for what felt like the tenth time, although it was probably only the third or fourth. Another watchman was writing it all down in a notebook.

Chief Magistrate Jabiru, huffing and puffing, because he was quite a fat man and fat men really shouldn't run up steep stairways, pushed his way through the crowd.

"Sorcerers!" he huffed. "Rock-folk! Sand-goblins! I don't believe a word of it. The boy's lying. He spends all his time with his nose in a book, can't tell fairy tales from the real world anymore. He must have been playing with a lamp and spilled oil on the altar. He knows he's not allowed to have a light in here at night, but do boys ever listen?"

"I didn't!" said Kokako, indignantly.

"As I thought! And you have the gall to admit it!"

"Admit what?"

"That you didn't listen!"

"I didn't spill oil! *You* listen to *me*! There was a sorcerer. Named Lord Barramundi. And goblins. They wanted to eat me! And one of the rock-folk. You know the stories say they're all molten rock inside, with a stone crust, and they flow along like lava from a volcano—well, look at the floor, look at that burnt trail. You can't believe I did that!"

One of the watchmen scuffed at the black streak on the floor and shrugged. "Probably just charcoal dust," he said.

"And there's no way I could have made a fire hot enough to burn a hole in the roof!" Kokako went on.

"So we're supposed to believe a sorcerer came in here and started a fire and burned up the *Oyon*, are we?" asked Chief Magistrate Jabiru. "We're not that stupid. You could at least have come up with a better story."

"Like lightning," said the woman in command of the city watch.

"What?" The chief magistrate looked at her.

"Lightning," said the commander. "Maybe lightning struck the roof and zapped the *Oyon* into dust."

"It's summer—the dry season, here in Keastipol at least," another magistrate said. She was from Yunitharrapol on the swampy north coast, where the summers were hot and rainy, and she often complained about how dusty Keastipol was, as if having your clothes grow mold was better.

The commander shrugged. "Could have happened. At least, lightning would be a better lie than saying a sorcerer did it, if the boy was going to lie, right?"

"So you think he's telling the truth?" Chief Magistrate Jabiru looked outraged that a mere watch commander would dare to argue with him.

The commander didn't seem to notice. She took off her bronze helmet to scratch her head. "Well, how do you know it wasn't lightning? Did you see it?"

"I couldn't see lightning that wasn't there."

"Ah, but you didn't see the boy drop a lamp, either."

"I didn't see his sorcerer, either!"

"Well, then, how do you know any of them are true?"

"They're not, that's my point!"

"So you don't believe the boy dropped a lamp?"

"I don't have to have seen it to know it's the only rational explanation. Stop arguing with me! I'm the chief magistrate! I demand you arrest him!"

"If you insist," the commander said. "But I think there should be some evidence of something. I'm pretty sure there's a law about that. Maybe we should go look it up."

"Good heavens, woman, look around you! This is the *Oyon*-Shrine. Do you see the *Oyon*?"

"No."

"Well, then, arrest him! Arrest him for … for treason! He destroyed the *Oyon*, the symbol of peace. He's trying to start a war. He's probably a spy for Paraburdupol or Irribiddipol or one of the other cities. They've always been jealous that the *Oyon* is kept here in Keastipol. Obviously he destroyed it for them!" The chief magistrate's voice was shrill with rage.

"I didn't!" Kokako shouted.

"Paraburdupol wouldn't destroy the *Oyon*!" cried the magistrate from that city. "It must have been Irribiddipol!"

"It wasn't us!"

"Wouldn't it have made more sense, if he was a spy, for him to have stolen it for another city?" asked the commander, interrupting what was turning into a good squabble among the magistrates. "I mean, destroying it wouldn't do anyone any good, would it?"

Maybe the commander truly thought it was wrong to arrest Kokako without any proof he'd committed a crime, or maybe she just wanted to argue with the chief magistrate for the fun of it. But either way, the commander was drowned out by a voice from the watching crowd.

"Traitor!"

That one shout seemed to set off a frenzy, like when sharks taste blood in the water.

"Thief!"

"He stole the *Oyon*!"

"He destroyed the *Oyon!*"

"He's half a foreigner, a Whenualander! He should never have been allowed to work in the *Oyon*-Shrine!"

"Get him!"

"Hey, hey, hey!" said the commander. "None of that! I guess I'd better take this boy into custody for his own safety, at least until ..."

But the crowd surged forward, shoving and shouting, and the watch were too slow to shove them back with the shafts of their tall spears. Someone grabbed Kokako by the arm and a woman whacked at him with a string bag full of fresh loaves of bread. Jix took off in a flurry of feathers. Kokako jerked free, covered his head with his arms, and bolted. Luckily, there were so many people they got in one another's way.

That didn't slow them down for long, though. Kokako raced out the door. The stairs—no, they'd see him. He turned to the left and went leaping down the steep hillside, over rocks and through scrubby wild olive trees that scratched his bare arms and legs.

"He went that way!" he heard a shrill voice scream. It was a voice he recognized. Delena the spider-duster. He glanced back. She stood at the top of the stairs, pointing ... pointing away to the right, into the grove of gum trees where the branches for the altar were cut. The crowd went roaring and shoving into the grove, with the helmets and spears of the watch bobbing along in the middle. For a brief moment, Delena looked down at Kokako. She winked, and then ran off after the rest of the crowd.

Kokako kept on running himself, heading for the busy city streets.

~~~~~

Unfortunately, it didn't take long at all for the crowd to search the gum tree grove and pour down into the city looking for him, spreading more rumors as they went. It was Chief Magistrate Jabiru who saw Kokako as he trotted down a side street, wondering where a good place to hide might be.

"There he is!" roared the magistrate. "Get him!"

Kokako didn't see any watchmen handy. If he had, he would have surrendered to them at once. At least if he were in jail,

he'd be safe, and he would have a trial, and no one would be able to prove he'd done anything wrong. But he didn't think he was going to get a trial if the mob caught him.

That's the thing about mobs. They stop being human and using their brains; they go into a mad frenzy, like sharks or crocodiles, and afterwards ... well, afterwards people might be sorry, but then it's too late and each person tries to make him- or herself feel better by saying, *Everyone else was doing it*. As though that's any sort of excuse.

Makes me glad I'm not human.

The crowd surged past the puffing, waddling magistrate. And again, Kokako ran. He ran and ran and ran, with no idea where he was going, where he could go, to be safe. Sweat poured down his face, stinging his eyes. His heart was pounding on the walls of his chest, trying to batter a way out. He had a stitch in his side, a horrible burning feeling in the muscles there, as if they simply couldn't stretch anymore.

Then he caught the toe of his sandal on an uneven stone and stumbled, landing on his hands and knees, skinning them on the rough cobbles of the street. He hardly noticed. Behind him, the mob roared like the waves on the shore. Kokako scrambled up and started running again. He dodged through the crowded market square, around pens of goats and sheep, tables of cheese, baskets of lemons, apples, figs, and onions, jugs of wine and olive oil, pails of cut flowers and rows and rows of little trees in pots, which were very fashionable for rooftop gardens that year.

People turned to watch him go, curious, but they didn't try to stop him, until somewhere behind him a voice shouted, "Get that boy! He's the one who burned down the *Oyon*-Shrine! He's the one who destroyed the *Oyon*!"

Kokako gulped down what was almost a sob, lowered his chin, and somehow forced his legs to move faster.

"Vandal!" a man shouted, almost in his ear, snatching at him.

"Traitor!" A woman with a basket of eggs balanced on her head caught him by the arm.

Kokako tore away and dodged around a stall where kebabs of garlicky mutton and eggplant on skewers roasted over a charcoal fire. His shoulder struck one of the thin poles holding up the stall's striped awning. He fell over and so did the pole. The kebab-seller yelled and flailed around under his fallen awning, trying to fight his way out. He struggled from beneath it—his enormous mustache bristling with anger—tripped over Kokako, and fell on top of the woman with the eggs. Her basket went flying. Kokako watched as the eggs soared through the air, tumbling, falling, exploding like slimy little bombs as they hit the cobblestones. For a moment, he almost wanted to laugh. But the awning was smoldering where it had fallen onto the charcoal brazier and the roasting kebabs. It burst into flame with a quiet *whoomp* sort of noise, and Kokako quickly crawled away between the legs of the gathering crowd while they were all distracted.

When he thought he was safe he stood up, and found his legs were shaking so badly he could barely walk, let alone run.

"Where'd that boy go?" he heard someone shouting. "Look what he did to my stall!"

"Over there! That way!"

"What'd he do?"

"He's the one who destroyed the *Oyon*!"

"Lock him up and throw away the key!"

"Take him to the harbor and throw him in the sea!"

Kokako didn't even have the breath to whimper. He put his head down and forced his shaking legs to run.

Then someone grabbed his arm again, and he didn't have the strength to fight; he just sagged where he was.

"Quick," said a voice. "Take this." And someone thrust a big clay flowerpot into Kokako's arms. It had several spiky-nee-dled little bunya trees planted in it, and it was heavy. He almost dropped it.

"And this." The person—a foreign girl several years older than Kokako—shoved another flowerpot at him. This one had a tall bluegum sapling in it. The long, leathery leaves smelled a bit like, well, a tomcat. Trying to balance the pots in his arms, Kokako ended up with his face full of reeking leaves.

"No, don't hold it down lower," said another, much deeper voice. "You want to hide your face. That's the point." Kokako couldn't see who was speaking at all.

"That's better," the girl said. "Come on. I'm hiring you to carry my shopping back to my ship."

Kokako sputtered. His mouth was full of bluegum leaves, which he didn't enjoy, not being a koala, and he could feel his knees trembling with exhaustion and the weight of the pots. Someone patted him on the back.

"Don't look around," said that deep voice again. "Just walk."

And somehow, Kokako managed to walk. He didn't look around. He followed the girl, staggering under the flowerpots and peering out through the leaves. She was quite a tall girl, with a long black braid, and she kept putting her hand to the hilt of her battered old sword, as though she were more nervous than she wanted to admit. She looked around at him once and smiled. Her eyes were bright in her sun-browned face, one blue, one green.

"Keep walking," she said quietly. "Here they come."

And suddenly there was a great mass of people around them, all yelling and clamoring.

"He went that way!"

"No, back up the hill!"

The kebab-seller tugged at the girl's sleeve. "Miss, miss, did you see a boy run by here? A nasty, evil-looking boy, a real villain?"

"Captain," the girl corrected him politely. "It's 'captain,' not 'miss.' And I haven't seen anybody run past me."

"Back up the hill, then!"

"Search every doorway!"

The whole crowd went pushing and jostling back the way they had come. When they were out of sight, Kokako took a deep, trembling breath.

The girl took the pot of bunyas away, leaving him carrying the tree that smelled like cat pee. But he wasn't going to complain. It had hidden his face completely from the mob.

"You'd better come back to *Shrike* and tell us what that was all about," she said.

Us? Kokako wondered. The only person he could see was the girl, the captain. But there had been that other voice, and the hand that had patted him on the back ...

He decided not to think about it. Sand-goblins and rock-folk and a sorcerer—why not an invisible person, too? Right then, invisible people were far less worrying than visible people who wanted to throw him into the harbor. Kokako took a firmer grip on the potted tree and trudged after the girl—the captain. He was almost sure he heard soft feet pattering alongside.

CHAPTER THREE

# In which Mirimick's laundry comes in handy

I don't think I've ever seen anyone look as scared as Kokako did, the first time I saw him. I didn't know his name then, of course. He was just this very frightened boy, running through the market. Anna and I had stopped to buy a snack from a kebab-seller, when Kokako came stumbling along, with all that stir and shouting behind him, and the egg-woman grabbed at him and the awning fell down ...

I thought at first that perhaps he was a thief, until I heard what people were shouting. Words like *vandal* and *traitor* and *throw him in the harbor*. I knew there had been a fire at the building they called the *Oyon*-Shrine the night before, and that a valuable relic had been destroyed. It was all that any citizen in the city would talk about that morning.

So when we saw Kokako for the first time and heard what people were shouting, it was fairly clear to both Anna and me that the screaming mob and the frightened boy and the fire were all connected. Of course, we didn't think that burning up the *Oyon*-Shrine and the *Oyon* was a good thing, but we didn't think throwing anyone into the harbor was, either. Anna and I didn't need to talk about it; we both hurried after the boy as soon as we saw him crawling away, and when we caught up with him, we hustled him off to the ship before he, or the mob chasing him, had time to think. Not that mobs ever take the time to think.

♈♈♈♈♈

"Quickly," said Anna, as soon as we were safely on *Shrike*'s deck. "Get out of sight—in there." She set the pot she carried down and took the other one from the boy, giving him a shove towards the door into the aftercastle, which on a cog like *Shrike* is the raised bit like a building at the rear, or stern. The captain's cramped little cabin was in the aftercastle, too.

The boy didn't move. For a moment I thought he was overwhelmed by the sight of all the laundry that was drying on clotheslines strung around the ship—some of the old lady pirates were surprisingly fond of flowery nighties, with lace and ribbons and everything—but then I realized he was staring up into the sky.

"Go on," said Anna. "Look, the city watch is coming down towards the harbor. Do you want them to find you again?"

"Wait!" said the boy, which was the first thing I had heard him say. "Jix is coming!"

"Who?"

Anna and I both looked around, but we didn't see anyone. Then there was a flashing, tumbling streak of color, and a parrot, all green and purple, with a red and yellow head, shot into the aftercastle and disappeared.

The boy seemed to see the distant gleam of the watch's helmets, then. He turned and dashed after the parrot.

"Mister Flytch!" Anna called. "Mirimick!"

Mister Flytch was the first mate, a big, dark, bald man with a bushy black beard. Mirimick, a little white-haired woman with a face like a pixie's, was the bow master, in charge of crossbows and archery—Shrike was still a fighting ship. Even honest merchants have to defend themselves.

"Sir?" asked Mister Flytch, waking up with a snort and peering down from the top of the forecastle, where he'd been sunbathing.

"Yes, Captain, dear?" asked Mirimick, popping up out of the hold like a chipmunk out of its burrow.

"We have a bit of a problem," said Anna. "At least we might, if those city watchmen are coming down here. They're after the boy."

"What boy?"

"The one in the aftercastle."

"There's a boy in the aftercastle?"

"What's he doing in the aftercastle?"

"Hiding," said Anna. "And I'd like to keep him hidden."

"Ah," said Mister Flytch. "Where's my sword, Mirimick?"

"You're wearing it," said the bow master, on her way to the

forecastle for a bow and arrows.

Mister Flytch looked, and saw that he was. He rubbed his eyes a bit sheepishly and said, "Hrmph."

Mirimick snickered, coming back with a regular bow, not a crossbow. A crossbow can shoot farther, but not so quickly as a simple bow—you want speed, if you're defending your ship against a crowd. "Nothing like a bit of a fight to wake you up, Flytch, but if you're not up to it, you can leave it to me."

Anna groaned. "Let's keep him hidden without starting a war with Keastipol, alright? We're only one small ship."

I agreed. All around the harbor were squat, round towers of gray stone, with catapults and ballistae (like giant crossbows) on their roofs, and big, curved, gilded bronze mirrors for focusing the sun's rays on the decks of ships and setting them on fire. They hadn't been used in a hundred years, but the people of Keastipol kept them all in working order anyway. Just in case.

"It's just in case, dear," said Mirimick, patting the bow and sounding a bit guilty. "I wouldn't want to have to repel boarders with a mop, and nearly all the crew's gone ashore to see the city." She thumped her foot on the deck and raised her voice. "Stand by for boarders, below!"

A pair of wrinkled, dark brown faces with clouds of curly, snow-white hair stuck up out of the hold: Banksy and Galeata, the ship's carpenters, had been down there working on some of our leaking seams. *Shrike* was an old ship, and we'd been through a lot of rough weather on the way to the Great Southern Continent. "Let 'em come," Galeata said, waving her hammer. "We're ready."

"No!" said Anna. "No fighting, even if they try to board us. Be clever instead."

Banksy shook his head. "That's not a good idea, Captain. We're not good at clever. Remember Flytch and the potato?"

"Don't mention the potato," growled Mister Flytch. You probably remember how he tried to trick the pirate-queen with a potato. It had almost ruined a good escape.

"Potato, potato," Mirimick sang softly,

Mister Flytch rapped her on the head with a knuckle. "It's alright, Captain. Trust us. We won't start a fight. Go talk to your new friend, before he burns the ship down, too."

So you see, it wasn't only Anna and I who could put two and two together. And Flytch didn't even know about the kebab stall.

≈≈≈≈≈

The boy was sitting on Anna's sea chest, looking very nervous and young, when we went into her cabin. The parrot was standing on his head. Kokako gave a sort of a squeak when he saw me, and the parrot fluffed his feathers out to make himself look bigger.

"Stay back, goblin!" he said, snapping his curved beak. "I've already dealt with one pack of goblins today. Tore 'em limb from limb!"

"Liar," I said cheerfully. He wasn't big enough to do that much damage to a goblin. "And I'm *not* a goblin."

I'd kept myself invisible to everyone but Anna, in the city. It causes fewer problems. I'm not human, as you can probably tell. I'm Torrie, the oldest of the Old Things of the Wild Forest. I'm about three feet tall, wiry and strong, not tubby, and covered in shaggy, rust-brown fur. I have yellow eyes and largish pointy ears and sharp teeth and a very dignified nose. And really, I don't think there's anything about me that should make people squeak when they see me, like they're a mouse that's just seen a cat. But I didn't know, then, that Kokako had barely escaped being eaten by goblins. *Not* that I look the *slightest bit* like a goblin.

"I'm Anna, captain of this ship, the *Shrike*," Anna said, pouring the boy a cup of water from the jug on the table. "And this is Torrie. He doesn't bite."

The boy took the cup in a hand that trembled with exhaustion. He was a bit steadier after he'd had a long drink.

"Kokako," he said hoarsely. "I'm Kokako. This is Jix."

The parrot puffed his feathers out again, until he looked about twice the size of a crow. "Jix the Terrible!" the bird said. "You watch it, goblin, or you're mincemeat."

I stuck out my tongue at him.

Anna poured Kokako some more water. He was obviously parched. He drank this cup more slowly. Anna watched him, nibbling on the end of her long braid in a thoughtful manner, no doubt wondering what she should do now that she'd rescued him.

Like most of the people of the Great Southern Continent, Kokako had nearly black skin and dark brown eyes. His hair was lighter brown and a bit curly. He was dressed in a short-sleeved white tunic, the kind that most people wear in all the cities of the Great Southern Continent, especially during the hot summers, which happen when we're having winter here in the Wild Forest.

Kokako's tunic was smeared with charcoal and there were ashes on his face and in his hair. His knees were oozy from falling on the stones, and he still smelled like smoke.

I handed him a damp towel, and he took it with a nod of

thanks, cleaning first his face, and then his knees.

"Would they really have thrown you into the harbor?" Anna asked.

"I didn't do it!" The words exploded. Jix gave a rasping sort of squawk and flapped his wings to keep his balance as Kokako jumped up. "It wasn't me! There was a sorcerer! And goblins! Honestly!"

"It's alright," I said reassuringly. "We're not going to let anyone throw you in the harbor."

Kokako gave me a look that suggested he was not at all reassured.

"What *are* you?" he asked.

"Torrie," I said. "Like she told you. An Old Thing."

"What's an Old Thing?"

I thought about that. "Old," I said finally. "Ancient. We were the First Things …"

"He's old," Anna interrupted. "Humans only see him when he wants them to. He can talk to animals. Iron and steel give him a rash." She gave me a stern look, to let me know this wasn't a good time for me to start explaining about how I wasn't a brownie, or a pixie, or a goblin, or any of the other sorts of Old Things that humans knew more about.

"You can talk to animals?" Kokako's face brightened. "Really? Then you can ask Jix. He'll tell you. He was there, the same as me."

The parrot croaked and hopped from foot to foot. "It's true," he said. "There was a man, and one of the rock-folk, and some sand-goblins. They made a huge fire. I nearly got barbecued. And they took the *Oyon*."

"They took it?" I asked. "People in the market were saying it was destroyed."

"They took something," Jix said. "What else was there to take? Kokako couldn't stop them, but I stopped the goblins, hah! You should have seen them run——"

"Yes, yes," I said.

I told Anna and Kokako what Jix had said, about the *Oyon* being stolen, not destroyed.

"I knew it!" Kokako said. "It just wouldn't make sense, if they'd burned it up. And the man disappeared, *whoomph*, did Jix tell you that? That's how I knew he was a sorcerer."

"You'd better tell us all about it," said Anna. "Have you had any breakfast? There's gingerbread in that jar, if you're hungry."

Galeata came in with tea for us all, her hammer stuck in her belt like a sword. So, while Kokako had a very late breakfast of tea and gingerbread (the old-fashioned kind that keeps forever, very useful on ships, not the squashy, cakey sort you're probably thinking of), we heard all about why Kokako lived in the *Oyon*-Shrine and what had happened there the night before. He had got up to the point where Anna shoved a potted tree at him when there were raised voices outside.

"No! You can't search the ship," came the deep roar of Mister Flytch. "The captain's taking a nap, and she'll be very cranky if she's disturbed. Anyway, I assure you, I've been here on the deck all morning and there haven't been any boys trying to stow away, I'd have seen 'em."

The other voice was quieter, so we couldn't hear what it said.

"I don't care what the laws of Keastipol say, you aren't setting foot on board *Shrike* while I'm standing here."

"Uh oh," said Anna, getting up. "I'd better get out there. Torrie, you hide Kokako."

Kokako hopped off the sea chest amd raised the lid, but it was stuffed full of books and charts and brass instruments for measuring the height of the stars. There wasn't a bed, only a hammock. Hiding under the table wouldn't do any good, and there certainly wasn't a closet.

Jix dove into the gingerbread jar and I put the lid on it.

"Turn me invisible, too!" Kokako said to me.

"I can't!" I said. "I'm not an enchanter."

"Just be quiet," said Anna, with her hand on the door, about to go out to meet the watchmen.

We all jumped as it opened and Mirimick struggled through, her arms piled high with still-damp washing off the lines.

"Don't mind me, just getting the laundry in!" she called loudly over her shoulder. Anna slipped out and shut the door firmly behind her.

"Get in the hammock!" I ordered.

"They'll see me," Kokako protested.

"No, they won't, lad," said Mirimick. "In you go."

Kokako scrambled into the canvas hammock, which is trickier than it sounds, as you'll know if you've ever actually slept in one, and Mirimick dropped her load of laundry on top of him. The next minute we heard Anna on the other side of the door saying, "Fine, you can search my ship, if it will make you happy, Commander. But be quick about it. My crew has work to do."

There was a suspicious munching noise from the gingerbread jar.

"Quiet!" I said.

"Hey, fighting goblins is hungry work!" said the jar. "And I didn't get any tea, either."

The door opened again, and several people from the city watch tromped in, treading on one another's heels, because it was a *very* small cabin. They looked rather grand, in an old-fashioned sort of way, with their bronze helmets and cuirasses —a cuirass is armor for your chest and back, with straps and hinges to hold it together. Mirimick pretended to be folding a shirt, humming to herself. I crawled under the table, where I wouldn't be walked on. In a small space, making yourself invisible doesn't always do much good. My own bronze-headed spear was propped in the corner, but Anna had said no fighting, so I left it there and hoped that cleverness was going to be enough.

"Right, no boys in here," said the woman I took to be the commander, since her helmet had a red crest on it and those of the others didn't. She turned to go, but one of her men reached out and prodded the heap of laundry.

"Shouldn't we check …?" he started to ask, but Mirimick slapped his hand.

"Keep your hands off of other people's undergarments!" she said. "The manners of some people's children!" The poor watchman looked horribly embarrassed and mumbled an apology. One of the watchwomen giggled.

"Go and check down in the hold," the commander told them severely, and they all trooped out again.

"By the way, Captain," the commander told Anna, stopping in the door so that Mirimick couldn't close it again, "you should be more careful about how many cups you pour when you're drinking tea all alone in your cabin."

And then she left, too.

That was when I realized that we'd left three half-drunk cups of tea sitting on the table.

I listened until I heard the watch leaving the ship, heading along the wharf to check the next vessel.

"All clear," I called. Anna came back in and Kokako popped up out of the heap of damp clothes.

"The commander doesn't really want to arrest me, but if she sees me, she'll have to," he said. "I'm going to have to leave Keastipol," he added forlornly. "Captain, can I sign on as crew?"

"If you're sure you want to," said Anna.

"You did say you wanted to be an explorer, Kokako," I pointed out, wondering why he sounded so dismal about it.

"But not on the ocean," he said quietly, and I remembered he had told us that his parents were both lost at sea.

"Oh," I said, and Anna made an understanding sort of noise.

"I wanted to explore my own land," he went on. "Especially the desert. No one's ever explored the whole desert."

It had been a long time since I had explored even a part of a desert, I thought. Now that I was here, I did want to see more of the Great Southern Continent than Keastipol, beautiful though the city was. And I still had that restless, adventurous feeling in my feet …

"You'll have some time to make up your mind, anyway," said Anna. "There are a lot of little repairs we have to make before we can sail again, and I need more than two pots of trees for my cargo. I don't want to buy them all in the market. It's too expensive to get a whole forest that way."

"Um …" I said, scratching the tip of my ear in a thoughtful sort of way. "Kokako, didn't you say the sorcerer told the sand-goblins to go to the salt lake?"

"Yes," said Kokako. "But I've never heard of a salt lake. And anyway, even if the commander of the watch half-believes me, she's not allowed to take her police outside the city. It's one of our laws that's supposed to prevent cities from starting wars. She couldn't go there to arrest the sorcerer, even if she knew where the salt lake was."

"But *we* can find it!" I said. "Why shouldn't we? I'm a master adventurer; it's just the sort of thing I do. We can find this salt lake and the sorcerer and figure out what happened to the *Oyon*! Anna can come, too," I added, because I had a feeling that if goblins were involved, a good swordswoman like her would come in handy.

I also had a feeling that this might not be a new adventure at all, but more of an old one. This wasn't the first time I'd run across a sorcerer who liked to have goblin servants …

"Anna can't come, too," said Anna, folding her arms. "Anna has a ship to look after and a cargo to find."

"Exactly!" I said.

Kokako, who looked much happier at the prospect of not going to sea, saw what I meant. "If there is a salt lake," he said, "it's probably out in the desert. And we'll have to go through the forest to get to the desert. You can collect, well, seeds and things, to plant later."

Anna frowned, tapping the end of her braid on her chin.

"And anyway, you're not a carpenter, Anna," I said. "Banksy and Galeata know what they're doing. Let them do it! You have to come with us. You're practically a master adventurer, like me."

"I'm a master *mariner*," she said, but I could tell she was tempted.

"And I can be your assistant adventurer," Kokako said eagerly. I almost think it was that, rather than all my rational arguments, that convinced her. He looked so young, leaning forward over the table. And he was so alone in the world. If he were ever to have a life in his own land again, he needed to clear his name, and the only way to do that was to find out what had actually happened to the *Oyon*.

"You'd better go, Captain," said Mirimick. "You don't know what sort of trouble Torrie might get Kokako into on his own."

I coughed. "I beg your pardon? I was having adventures when you were in diapers, Mirimick."

"You're right, Mirimick," Anna said. "If I let Torrie and Kokako go off alone, I'll just spend the whole time worrying about them." She gave me a bit of a defiant look, but I wasn't going to argue that I could look after Kokako on my own after all and didn't need her to worry about me. I grinned. The truth was, there was a part of Anna that had itchy, adventuring feet, too.

The gingerbread jar rocked violently back and forth, and then tipped over. The lid fell off and Jix marched out, clacking his beak.

"I'm coming, too," he said. "You'll need me if you meet goblins."

"What happened to all my gingerbread?" Anna asked sternly. Jix was drinking tea out of Kokako's cup. He flipped his tail at her, quite rudely.

# CHAPTER FOUR

# In which crocodiles don't keep promises

A nd so it was settled; Anna and I would go with Kokako to look for the salt lake and the sorcerer who had either stolen or destroyed the *Oyon*. What we would do then depended on what we found. It can be a mistake to make detailed plans too far ahead, I always think.

Banksy and Galeata, the ship's carpenters, were both originally from the Great Southern Continent. They were very suspicious of Kokako at first. After all, the *Oyon* was important to all seventy of the cities, even the one they were from in the farthest west, that you could get to only by sailing right around to the other side of the continent. If Kokako really had destroyed the *Oyon*, I'm afraid Banksy and Galeata would have agreed he should be thrown in the harbor. At least they had the excuse of being pirates. But Kokako's own honesty soon persuaded them and, of course, having sailed with me, they weren't that surprised at stories of sand-goblins and sorcerers. They gave us lots of advice on what sorts of supplies we were likely to need. Banksy even thought he had heard stories of a salt lake, somewhere between the Dandarigan and the Gunyidy Deserts, away to the northwest. If he were right, we knew which direction we should go once we crossed the mountains.

Mister Flytch thought it was a bad idea, but he always did think it was a bad idea whenever Anna took risks. He argued, but in the end, she was the captain.

Actually, I think part of what made him give in was Mirimick whispering loudly behind her hand to Kokako, "It's not his fault, poor dear. Old age has made him get all responsible. Sometimes it happens that way, you know—one moment you're the terror of the seas, and the next you're an old mother hen."

We set out in the early hours of the morning, before the sun was up. Both the humans carried packs of supplies, and even I had a water gourd slung over my shoulder, as well as my spear. There would be lots of water in the forests, but once we were into the desert, waterholes would be few and far between. Even an immortal Old Thing like me needed water. The desert wasn't my proper place. But adventures don't happen, if you just stay home.

"Good-bye!" we wished the crew, and "Good-bye!" they called after us. "Good luck, Captain!"

"Behave yourselves," Anna called back. "No piracy while I'm gone, Flytch."

"Wouldn't dream of it, Captain," he said.

"Do you have your fingers crossed?" I asked.

Mister Flytch grinned, and held up both hands. "Never!" he said, and then winked. "I might have crossed my toes, though."

Mirimick gave the first mate an elbow in the ribs. "I'll keep him in line, Captain, dear," she said. "Torrie, you just make sure you bring them back safely."

"Aye, aye!" I said.

And we were off.

Our plan was to travel north along the coast for several days, keeping to back roads and trails, until we were far enough from Keastipol that no one would recognize Kokako. Then we would get onto one of the main roads that headed inland, through the Fengu Forest, over the Mundaring Mountains, and to the sheep farms of the Bookabee Highlands on the western side of the mountains. From there, we would continue down to the Dandarigan Desert and turn towards the north again, where, we hoped, we could find the salt lake Banksy the carpenter had heard about.

And then what? We didn't know what Lord Barramundi wanted with the *Oyon*. We didn't know if he had in fact stolen it, or if it had been burned up in the fire. We didn't even know for certain there was a salt lake at all.

Well, I'd think of something. I always do.

Even though Kokako had lived most of his life in the city, he turned out to know quite a lot about the landscape we traveled through. It came from all the reading he'd done. Anna collected seeds for Prince Frederik along the way, and she couldn't have done it without Kokako—at least, she couldn't have done it as well. Usually Kokako could tell her the name of the tree, and Anna would put the seeds in a tiny cloth bag and label it, and write down in her notebook what sort of place that tree liked to grow. It was all very scientific. Kokako and Jix kept trying to outdo one another in finding new kinds of trees for her.

One afternoon, they went running ahead because Jix said he had found a kind of mangrove tree that Anna hadn't collected seeds from yet.

"Be careful!" Anna shouted after them, for about the tenth time that day. We'd already had to rescue Jix when he'd gotten tangled up in some sort of creeper, and Kokako had been stung by bees twice and fallen out of more trees than I could count.

Kokako waved cheerfully, pretending he hadn't heard that, and disappeared down the narrow path. It was slick and slippery with mud. We were crossing a shallow inlet where a sluggish river broadened out into the sea. The inlet was full of twisted trees with roots rising like bent knees out of the muck and water. Sometimes the path ran along mud, sometimes it clambered over knotted roots, and sometimes it crossed the shallow, silty water on a rickety boardwalk of rotting timbers, probably built by the people who came into the swamps to trap crayfish and crabs. Goggle-eyed mudskippers lay propped on their front fins on the mud, staring at us in astonishment as we passed, before they went zipping away among the tangles of roots. It was hard to believe they were truly fish, and not some sort of peculiar lizard. Storks flapped away from us, their gangly legs trailing, and black swans stretched out their long necks and hissed.

We heard a distant splash and a shout.

Anna shook her head and laughed. "Now Kokako's fallen *in*."

There was more shouting, and a screech that might have been Jix.

Anna and I looked at one another and started to run.

Racing around the turn, we came to a sudden halt, slithering on the last few broken planks of the boardwalk. Ahead of us was a broad expanse of murky water, choked with dark mangroves. Kokako was dangling from a branch, kicking his legs, trying to get up on top of the limb to which he clung. He must have been trying to cross the water by clambering from one tangle of arched roots to another.

The water swirled and I saw why he was so desperate to get up on the branch. A great, brownish, nubbly-scaled head broke the surface and heaved a long, bulky body out after it. A huge jaw snapped in the air.

"Dragon!" I screamed, and I charged into the water with my spear raised to my shoulder, ready to throw. The water only came up to my waist, but my feet sank in the deep mud and I could only flounder noisily. I sprang up onto a floating log and ran along it instead.

"Not a dragon!" panted Kokako. "Crocodile!"

I'd been wondering why it hadn't roasted him already.

"Hold on, Kokako!" Anna shouted, springing from one clump of roots to the next.

The log I was running along suddenly reared up out of the water. I have an excellent sense of balance, but I wasn't expecting that. I pitched forward and flung my arms around its great jaws. It twisted, lashing the water with its tail, but it couldn't get its mouth open.

"Stop that!" I told it. "Stop it or I'll stab you." That would be difficult, since I had dropped my spear in the shallow water.

The crocodile lay still, rolling eyes like dead, yellow stones, to glower at me.

"I'm going to let you go," I said. "If you promise not to eat us."

The crocodile looked sullen. I took that as a yes, and released it.

There was a frenzied splashing behind me and I whirled around to see yet another crocodile charging through the water, heaving itself forward like a battering ram over the back of the one I was, well, riding, I suppose.

Its pink mouth gaped wide enough to swallow me whole.

Anna sprang from the nearest tangle of roots and swung at it with every ounce of her strength. It swept its heavy tail at her, and she leapt over it, striking again, twice more. With her last blow, she cut off its head. Feeling a bit fluttery in my stomach, I grabbed up my spear again.

Kokako, meanwhile, had managed to scramble up on top of the branch.

"Look out," he called breathlessly. "There's more coming!"

He was right. There were five or six more swimming up, their great bodies wriggling back and forth just below the surface of the water. The first one, the biggest, twenty-five feet long if it was an inch, still circled beneath Kokako's tree.

Anna steadied herself with a hand on my head as we stared around us. Then I remembered we were still standing on a crocodile. The crocodile remembered, too.

*"Geroff,"* it growled, as one of the new crocodiles came darting in to attack, not us, but the one we were standing on. Anna jumped away to the clump of roots, and I followed her.

Crocodiles have no sense of fellowship. They didn't care that we'd killed one; they were just going to fight, to see who got to eat us. My crocodile, if I can call it that, was in the middle of the brawl.

"You promised not to eat us!" I called to remind it. "Help us get away!"

"Didn't promise," it said, appearing for a moment above the thrashing tangle of reptiles. "Going to eat you."

"You did so promise," I said.

"I don't think it could have promised, actually," Kokako called from several trees away, where he was carefully picking his way up to a higher branch. "I mean, you were holding its mouth shut, weren't you, Torrie?"

"It nodded," I said. Well, it might have.

"Didn't," said the crocodile. Another one flipped it over and a great wave of muddy water drenched Anna and me. "Mine!" it roared, flinging itself back into the fight.

"Mine!" bellowed another. The smallest crocodile grabbed the tail of the one Anna had killed and started dragging it away to eat, and the biggest one decided that since Kokako was out of reach, it was going to join the fun. It came swimming back towards us.

I realized that day that I don't like crocodiles one bit.

"Hey!" I shouted. "Look there! A huge fat wildebeest!"

The battling crocodiles ignored me.

"We don't have any wildebeests on the Great Southern Continent!" Kokako called.

"A huge fat ... sheep!" I said. "A whole flock of sheep. Look!"

"Where sheep?" bellowed one of the crocodiles, scrabbling up over the others and swinging its heavy head around.

"There! Down that way! They're swimming out towards the sea!"

The crocodiles were deadly, ravenous, *stupid* animals. They all went arrowing off through the water in the direction I pointed. The last I saw of them was a line of ripples, heading for the sea. Anna and I scrambled along, jumping and wading and climbing, and Kokako came down and joined us. Once we were safely on the trail again, beyond the section where the boardwalk had washed out, we started running.

We hurried along in silence for a while.

"There aren't *supposed* to be crocodiles here," Kokako said at last, as though he found it somehow insulting that his books could be wrong. "They must have come down from the north coast. Annapurna Khanum says they can swim for hundreds of miles at sea."

"Well, I pointed them in the right direction, then," I said. "Um, Anna, are you all right?"

Anna had made a strangled, *gurk* sort of noise and stopped running. We both piled into her.

"*Who* did you say?" she asked Kokako.

"Annapurna Khanum. The explorer. She says—well, not to me personally, I mean, I've never met her. But in her book "Swamps, Lagoons, and Stringybarks," about the north coast, she says crocodiles can …"

Anna made that *gurk* noise again. "I've never *heard* of that one!" she snapped indignantly, as though not having heard of it was somehow Kokako's fault.

"Well, I think she only wrote it last year," Kokako said, looking at Anna a bit worriedly.

"I didn't even know she was *in* the Great Southern Continent," Anna went on.

Kokako and I looked at one another. "Um," I said. "Why should you have known?"

"She's my mother," Anna said.

There was a long pause. Kokako and I looked at one another again. Then we both looked at Anna.

"I thought your mother was dead," I said bluntly. That wasn't really a kind way to say it, but since Anna had never talked about her in all the time we sailed together, I'd simply assumed …

"Dead? No! She isn't dead. She's just … she's a bit … um, difficult, I suppose."

"Difficult how?" I asked, wondering how a mother could

be difficult. I don't have much experience with mothers, never having had one myself.

Anna tugged on her braid. "Difficult. Oh, you know, frustrating, sometimes. Aggravating. Sometimes I just want to pick her up and shake her and yell, 'Hey, pay attention to us! We need you, too!' Except, of course, she's taller than me, so I can't." Anna laughed at the look on my face as I tried to imagine this. "I guess you could say she has itchy feet. Like you, Torrie. She never can stay put. Always off traveling somewhere. Exploring. 'Bye, dears, see you when I get back,' and she disappears for a year or two, and my father and I never know where she's going or where she's been, until she does get back." A frown crossed her face, a bit angry, a bit sad. "But it doesn't mean she doesn't love us, we know that. You know, like being a sailor with a family that stays ashore. If you're a sailor, you have to go to sea, and if your husband or your wife is a farmer or a professor or something, well, obviously they have to stay on the land. You're not apart because you're angry or you've stopped caring about your family; it's just what you have to do, to be yourself—and to make a living, of course."

Kokako nodded. He, at least, understood about that sort of family, as well as Anna did.

"I suppose she's too used to always traveling to ever stay still. We couldn't expect her to stop wandering any more than you could expect the geese not to fly north in the spring. Her mother, my grandmother, is a singer. She's always traveling, too, and even when my mother was a baby, Grandmother would leave her with her friends, all over the world, while she went off on her own. I guess there weren't any other relatives to look after her, except an uncle, and my grandmother doesn't get along with him at all. When I was little, I thought there was some terrible secret about him, but I've never found out what it is." Anna laughed again. "Mother calls him her Wicked Uncle, like in fairy tales. But when you think about Father's side of the family being pirates and all, I don't see what my great-uncle could have done that would be so bad."

"But——" said Kokako. He shook his head, and I realized it was awe that had been keeping him quiet. "Your mother is Annapurna Khanum. *Annapurna Khanum!* And you never said."

"Well, it's not like she's the queen or something," Anna said, amused.

But he still stared, as if Anna had suddenly grown a golden halo.

I decided not to explain that "Khanum" wasn't a name, but a title that meant something like "Lady" in Callipepla. Kokako didn't look as if he needed to be any more impressed, although, since the cities of the Great Southern Continent were all republics without aristocrats, maybe he wouldn't have been. Instead, I gave them both a poke in the ribs. "Crocodiles," I reminded them. "Let's get out of this swamp." The boardwalk wasn't nearly high enough out of the water for my liking.

We all started jogging again, the humans' packs thumping on their backs.

"Anna," panted Kokako. "But Anna, you must have——do you get to read her books while she's writing them?"

"Get to?" Anna asked. "She used to make me correct her

spelling! I used to climb to the top of the mast to hide. Well, when she was sailing with Father and me. She didn't write on the ship very often, because her handwriting's bad enough as it is, without the ship swaying around making it worse. We do have a house, you know, a little cottage in Erythroth. Usually she stays there to write. That's about the only time she does come home, when she's done exploring some place and wants to start a new book about it. Although obviously not this time." To me, those last few words sounded a bit angry again.

"Well," Kokako suggested. "It is a long way from here to Erythroth. Maybe she wasn't done exploring here yet."

"Maybe," Anna admitted. "But she could have let us know." Then she sighed. "It's just the way she is. She doesn't realize how much Father worries, and he won't tell her because he doesn't want her to feel like she should be staying home, or that she lost her freedom by getting married. Although I think she ought to consider his feelings a bit more, too."

"And yours," I pointed out.

Anna gave me a crooked smile over her shoulder. She simply wasn't the sort to sit around feeling sorry for herself at all. "I suppose so, yes. But then, you know, Torrie, she takes it for granted that my father and I should have as much freedom as she does. She's never complained about me going off sailing with Father, the way I have been practically ever since I could walk." She looked thoughtful. "I did get angry about her leaving, when I was little. It turned into a real tantrum once, screaming and crying and kicking the doorframes, you know. And I was angry with my father, too—I thought he should make her stay and sail on *Oriole* with us. He said, 'Maybe she should make us go with her to find the lost city of the Pearl River Delta,' and I said, 'We can't do that, we have a cargo to deliver,' because even then I was trying to be a proper merchant sailor, and he said, 'Yes, you're right, we do. And she's got a lost city to find.' It really made me think." She shrugged. "So even if I start to feel a bit—well, angry—and sometimes I do, then I try to remember that. Even when I think it would be nice if she spent more time with Father and me. She doesn't want to be in a cage any more than either of us do. And at least I know she won't be upset, and say I'm too young or too inexperienced to captain my own ship now, even though most people my age don't have their master mariner's papers yet and are still apprentices or junior mates."

Kokako wasn't listening to all this. "Annapurna Khanum," he whispered to himself, as though the name was some sort of magical incantation, and he bit his tongue as he stumbled on a rough bit of boardwalk. "Ow! Anna? Do you think I could, um, write her a letter, sometime? Would you give it to her?"

Anna gave a snort of laughter. "Sure. But don't get your hopes up. It could be a few years before she remembers to come home again."

Kokako fell silent. From the way his lips moved occasionally, shaping a word, trying it out, I think he was mentally composing a letter to Annapurna Khanum.

We didn't dare stop for a real rest until we were out of the mangroves and back on dry land, where the tall, airy eucalypts towered over us again. Jix caught up with us there, tumbling down out of the sky with a whirring of wings.

"There you all are," the parrot said. "That was some fight, eh, Torrie? Did you see me attacking those crocodiles?"

"No," I said.

"I dove at them. I clawed them. I chased them out to sea."

"I didn't see a single feather," I said.

"Well, I did."

"Sure."

Jix hopped from foot to foot and nibbled at Kokako's hair. "I wasn't hiding in a tree or anything."

"You'd never do a thing like that."

"Anna," said Kokako, after we'd walked a bit more, and our hearts had all slowed down to something like their normal rates.

"What?" Anna asked, looking back at him. She looked as if she were braced for more questions about her mother.

Kokako grinned at her. "It's alright, I'm not going to ask anything more about Annapurna Khanum. I wanted to say, the way you cut that crocodile's head right off …"

"I didn't have any choice," Anna said. "It was going to kill Torrie."

"But you just jumped right at it." He was still looking at her with a bit of something like awe in his eyes. "And the way Torrie grabbed that other one … and all I could do was sit there in the tree yelling like a baby. Do you master adventurers do that sort of thing all the time?"

"Not if we can help it," I said. It was sort of an accident, my tripping, although I didn't want to admit it.

"Can you teach me?" he asked Anna, as if I hadn't spoken. I sighed.

Anna grinned at me over his head, and tugged on her braid. "You don't have a sword."

"Well, I could use a stick, to practice."

"A spear might be a better weapon for you," I suggested. "When you're small, like me, you don't want to get in close enough to big dangerous things like crocodiles to use a sword."

"He's quite a lot bigger than you, Torrie," Anna pointed out.

"Not *that* much bigger."

"Yes," said Kokako. "But *I'm* going to grow."

There wasn't anything I could say to that. It was true.

# CHAPTER FIVE

# In which one of us disappears

After the crocodiles, we followed a good road heading inland towards the Mundaring Mountains. News of the disaster in Keastipol had traveled even faster than us, and from others on the road we heard either that the citizens of Keastipol had hidden the *Oyon* so as not to share it with the other cities, or that a terrible spy, a seven-foot-tall hunchback who was practically an ogre, had burned down the *Oyon*-Shrine and destroyed the *Oyon*. People who told the first story said that the other cities were going to send their city guards and militias to tear Keastipol apart to find it, while those who repeated the second rumor said that Keastipol was going to send its guard to punish whatever city the spy came from, as soon as they figured it out.

Either way, it seemed as though the loss of the *Oyon* was going to start another time of war between the cities. It seemed to me that the people of the Great Southern Continent believed that the giant opal had been the actual peace, and not merely the symbol of it.

Nobody, not even travelers from Keastipol, recognized Kokako. I suppose he simply didn't look like a sweeper any more, which might have been because he wasn't carrying a broom or being chased by a mob. Of course, it could have been because he wasn't a seven-foot-tall hunchbacked ogre, either.

Aside from the talk of punishing this or that city, it would have been easy to forget we were on a desperate quest to clear Kokako's name. We traveled through the Fengu Forest, which wasn't dark and dense overhead like my home in the Wild Forest, but open and airy, with all the different kinds of tall gum trees stretching for the sky like great columns, their leaves making a lacy, gray-green or green-blue canopy far above. Beneath them, our road wound among ferns and shrubs; some of the bushes were still flowering yellow and red, and the air smelled like spice and honey. Down in the ravines, where narrow brooks ran, the undergrowth was much greener and denser, harder to get through, and full of small birds.

We kept on, heading through the rising hills towards the low blue mountains in the west. At home, we'd have just called them hills. They don't know what real mountains are like, there on the Great Southern Continent.

Every night, Kokako had a lesson in sword-fighting from Anna, using sticks. As we walked along during the day, he was always leaping at bushes and shadows, practicing. I thought it was doing him good. He didn't fall out of trees or trip over

things nearly so often.

Then I awoke one morning to find I was alone by the ashes of last night's fire.

"Anna?" I asked, sitting up.

No Anna.

"Kokako?"

No Kokako.

"Jix?"

"I'm asleep."

"You are not," I said, going over to the roosting parrot and poking him with my spear. "Where are they?"

"Who?" Jix asked, in a muffled sort of voice, with his head twisted around and his beak nestled between his folded wings.

"The humans."

"Oh, them." Jix raised his head and shook his feathers, stretching first his right wing and leg, and then his left, yawning.

"Parrots," I said sternly, "are supposed to get up at dawn. Every other parrot in this forest gets up at dawn. Noisily. What's wrong with you?"

"Nothing," said Jix indignantly. "I like to sleep in. I think I've got a bit of night parrot in me."

"You do not," I said. "Look, you can fly, go find the humans. Something's happened to them."

Jix yawned again. "Nothing's happened to them. They went off to climb some tree your captain saw last night." He blinked and clacked his beak. "Er, I wasn't supposed to tell you that, I think."

"What? Why?" But Jix had snuggled his beak back into his feathers and was pretending to be asleep.

I shook my head and went to find Anna and Kokako. After a moment, Jix flew after me.

It didn't take me long to find the humans. First I heard someone saying, "Look out! Be careful!" and then I heard someone, rather higher up, saying, "I am being careful!"

"Hi, Torrie!" Kokako said, looking a bit guilty when he saw me. "Um, we're just … I mean, Anna wanted … I said maybe it was too high but she …"

Kokako, at least, still had both his feet on the ground. I tilted back my head and looked up. Way up. The tree had a streaky white trunk, and no branches at all on the lower part, only a few knobby places. It was about as wide as the height of a tall man at the base, rising like a spire above all the other trees around, and the rest of them were pretty tall, too.

"Anna said it was such a good tree she had to get seeds from it," Kokako said, still sounding guilty. "I told her …" Then he couldn't help himself, and he bounced up and down on his toes, pointing. "Isn't she great?"

"Why," I asked carefully, feeling like I was about as old as— well, I am as old as the hills. But usually I don't feel it. "Why didn't you just send Jix up to knock some seeds down?"

"He's always so cranky first thing in the morning."

"Tell him that's because people are always waking me up before I'm ready," Jix grumbled.

I looked up at Anna. This tree was much, much higher than any ship's mast. She was sitting astride the lowest branch, surrounded by circling, squawking green parrots, and bigger gray and pink ones, and she was stretching, carefully, to pick the seeds.

"Maybe you could, um, do some magic. You know, zap a branch with a firebolt and make some seeds fall down," Kokako suggested hopefully. "Before Anna does."

"I'm not a sorcerer," I said, with, I think, great dignity. "We Old Things don't do that sort of flashy magic."

"I haven't noticed that you do any magic," said Jix.

I ignored him. Parrots aren't known for their manners.

Anyway, it's often difficult to explain to humans and animals the difference between Old Thing magic and human sorcery, especially when some Old Things, like the Fair Folk, go around doing flashy sorcery all the time, just to show off. For Old Things, true magic is rooted deep in our place in the world. Of course, we can do little things, like wish people to be well, and go unseen to human eyes, but our real strength is in our land; it's deep and powerful, like a flood or an avalanche, when we do turn it loose. But we really, really try hard not to. It's not like our purpose in the world is to make things easy for humans who ought to be figuring out how to solve their own problems.

We don't do zappy firebolts. Not usually, anyhow.

"Hold this," I said, handing Kokako my spear. I flexed my fingers and toes a few times to limber up, and then I headed up the tree myself. Like a squirrel, but a bit more slowly.

"Hey," I said, once I had joined Anna on her branch. "This was stupid. You'll die if you fall from this height. And then what would Mister Flytch say to me?"

"Well, I certainly wasn't going to let Kokako climb up here," she said, putting a last few seeds in her pocket.

The flocks of parrots circled closer, shouting things like "Thief!" and "Trespassers!"

"Anyway, look at the view, Torrie! Isn't this worth it?" Anna waved a hand, chasing off some parrots and indicating a great sweep of forest below.

I looked out over miles and miles of gray-green treetops rasping and whispering in the wind, the occasional silver flash of water, the swirling flocks of brightly colored birds, the Mundaring Mountains rising hazy blue. Another day or two and our road would be taking us up into them. It took my breath away.

"Yes," I said. "I think the view is worth it." Then I pointed. "Do you have your telescope, Anna? What's that?"

Anna felt around in the pocket of her coat and pulled out her telescope. I steadied her as she put it to her eye and looked where I was pointing, at a thin dark line wandering through the open ground between the trees.

"It looks like there's been a fire," Anna said slowly. "It's all black and charred. But forest fires don't burn in narrow paths."

"Kokako said the rock-man left a burn on the floor of the *Oyon*-Shrine."

"I don't actually know what a rock-man is," Anna admitted.

"Me neither. I don't think we have rock-folk in the Wild Forest. But we'd better go and see what this path is."

"Hey!" shouted Kokako from below. "What are you doing up there? Are you stuck? Do you want me to come up and help you down?"

"No!" we both shouted, and very carefully we climbed down, Anna with a rope looped around herself and the tree, so she had something to brace herself against. It was only as safe as her knots. But then, she was a sailor, and if there's one thing sailors know, it's how to tie a good knot. I still found it awfully hard to watch. Looking after these young people can be very stressful, I tell you.

After breakfast, we packed up and set off towards that dark, burnt trail, walking in single file, weaving through the undergrowth. I could smell the burnt earth—dry and metallic instead of warm and sweet and spicy—long before Anna, who was leading the way with her compass in her hand, called out, "Here we are."

One by one, we emerged onto a barren track. The branches closest to it were withered or even singed, and the ground was baked hard, almost like clay that has been fired to make bricks. The breeze raised little puffs and swirls of ash.

"A very strange fire," Anna said, scraping at the ground with her sword. The crust of baked clay was very thin, and broke into pieces easily. The forest would start to grow back when the winter rains came.

"It was one of the rock-folk," Kokako said, with confidence. "All the books say that when they move quickly, they scorch the earth."

"Why do they scorch the earth?" Anna asked.

"Because they're made of rock," Kokako answered. "Or lava, I think. And they don't have feet. They sort of—ooze—like a, a, a …"

"A slug?" I suggested. It was the ooziest thing I could think of.

"I suppose." Kokako scratched his chin. "They're tall, though, not long like a slug."

What I imagined then was a snowman made of stone, rolling forward with his crust cracking and grinding, letting the heat of a volcano out onto the earth. Actually, though, rock-folk look a bit more like termite mounds.

"Are there a lot of these rock-folk around?" Anna asked practically.

"I don't know. They're supposed to live in the mountains, mostly, but the books say they're legends." Kokako grinned. "You know, like sand-goblins and things like Torrie."

"You mean *Things*," I said. "You have to say *Things* like it matters. With dignity. What do you think, Anna? Should we follow it?"

It was Kokako who answered. "Of course we should! It was working for the sorcerer!"

"You don't know if this is the same one," Anna said. She was tapping the end of her braid on her chin as she spoke, so I could tell she was thinking.

"But——" Kokako began.

Anna held up a hand. "And, Torrie and I could see quite a lot of this track from up in that tree. It twists and wanders all over the place. It is heading towards the mountains, but if we follow it, we could easily take another week to get as far as we would travel in a couple of days on the road. So I think we should go back to the straight road. We need to find the salt lake and the sorcerer; that's the most important thing."

"But——" began Kokako again.

"We might be able to learn something from this rock-man," I pointed out. I wasn't arguing with Anna, I was just making sure she had thought of this, too.

She had. "I know," she said. "But that's *if* it's the one Kokako saw, and *if* we can catch up with it, and *if* it'll talk to us, and *if* it knows anything. Those are a lot of *ifs*."

"So we go back to the road," I said.

"We do."

"Aye aye, Captain."

Kokako looked disappointed, but he didn't complain, and pretty soon he and I were running ahead, taking swipes at one another with long flower stalks of some plant that looked a bit like rhubarb.

"Keep your weight balanced!" Anna called at Kokako. I think it was at Kokako. She broke off a stalk for herself and came charging after us. "On guard!" So shouting and laughing and dueling with one another, we all tumbled back out onto the road, and didn't think about the rock-man anymore.

At least, Anna and I didn't.

～～～～～

Our way rose into the mountains, keeping to high ridges, angling along steep cliffs over which small rivers tumbled in roaring plumes of white spray. From the tangled green ravines rose the calls of strange birds (mostly, it seemed to me, about a hundred different kinds of parrot, but that might have been because they were the loudest). On the heights, the forest grew thinner, gradually turning into scattered trees and groves, and the air became pleasantly cool for Anna and I, although Kokako shivered and wrapped himself in his cape.

One evening we reached a lofty saddle of land, from which we could look back over the way we had come, down the long fall of the mountains to the forest shimmering below like a cloud. The sun was setting, and the dark shadows poured over the lower hills, rushing towards the east. In the last light, I saw the scorched track of the rock-man again, following the course of the road only a few hundred yards from our camp.

I decided that investigating it could wait until morning. It was late, I was hungry, and Anna had promised to make pancakes.

That was probably a mistake. Not the pancakes. I mean the waiting.

We had our pancakes, and then, because we had been climbing all day and that's tiring even for master adventurers like us, we all rolled up in our blankets around the fire and went right to sleep.

"It should be all downhill, starting tomorrow," Anna remarked, and that was the last thing I heard that night.

～～～～～

I thought I was the first one to wake up, with the dawn chorus of birds and the bright glare of the rising sun. I picked up the kettle and went to get water from a nearby spring, before I realized someone was missing. Kokako was gone.

And so, as I saw when I went to shake Anna awake, was Anna's sword.

CHAPTER SIX

# In which Kokako asks some questions

Kokako tossed and turned and just couldn't get comfortable. First there was a stone under his back; then there was a prickly plant under his ear; then his blanket was too scratchy. The real problem, he had to admit to himself, was that his mind wouldn't settle down and rest. His thoughts kept niggling and nagging him.

For Anna and Torrie, he thought, this was probably just an adventure, an expedition into a strange country. They didn't have to take it seriously. For him, the adventure was deadly serious. All his life, Kokako had heard stories about the long years when city fought city and people hardly dared travel beyond sight of their own walls. Without the *Oyon*, those bad old days would return.

Torrie and Anna, Kokako thought, didn't *understand*. If they did, they would have hunted down that rock-man and made him (or her, if it turned out to be a rock-woman) answer some questions about the sorcerer. It was all very well heading for the desert and hoping to find the salt lake, but that could take weeks. Months. And all the time the Great Southern Continent might be arguing its way towards war.

He'd seen the track of the rock-man again that evening, while he was collecting firewood, but since neither Torrie nor Anna had pointed it out, he didn't think they'd noticed.

Maybe it was time he did something himself.

He had taken a good look at the rock-man's path, and the wilted leaves and grasses alongside it had looked quite recently withered, not all crumbled away yet. The creature might be quite close. It probably wouldn't usually travel as fast as it had in the *Oyon*-Shrine—if it did, it should be hundreds of miles away by now, not leaving fresh ashy tracks here.

And there was still that lumpy stone under his back.

Kokako got up and put on his sandals and his cape. He tied a water-gourd to his belt, because tracking might be thirsty work. And, his heart pounding, he slid Anna's sword in its scabbard away from her hand, and fastened it to his own belt. After all, he told himself, she would have Torrie and his spear to protect her. He didn't know what he might run into on the mountaintop. Besides, he'd be back by morning.

In case he wasn't, he knelt down and poked Jix until the parrot twitched and opened half an eye.

"I'm going to find the rock-man," Kokako whispered, with his nose almost in Jix's feathers. "If I'm not back by morning, tell Torrie I said they should follow the trail, too."

"*Gerr-wup,*" Jix mumbled. His eye closed again. He snuggled his beak more firmly into his feathers and stood on his left foot instead of his right.

Anna was sleeping with her head pillowed on her arm. In the silvery moonlight, she looked very pale, more like a ghost than a person. She also looked very young, and for a moment, Kokako felt quite guilty about going off on his own. He almost woke her up. But he didn't. Torrie was curled up in a tight furry ball like a cat, snoring.

∿∿∿∿∿

So Kokako claims. I *never* snore.

∿∿∿∿∿

It was easy to see the scorched trail in the moonlight. Kokako hitched the sword a bit tighter in his belt and started jogging along the trail, his feet stirring up puffs of ash.

He enjoyed the sensation of running, all his hard new muscles from hiking and climbing and sword-drill, stretching and springing. This was the life he wanted, exploring the land. When he got home to Keastipol, he'd start writing a book about his travels, like Annapurna Khanum did. He still found it hard to believe she was a real, ordinary person, someone's mother. Although probably Anna often wished her mother were more ordinary, and would stay home with her family. Still, if everyone were ordinary, interesting things would never happen, great things would never be done. Someday he'd do great things, like Anna and her mother. He wasn't going to stop exploring after one adventure, not a chance.

The sky behind him grew paler, and the first lemon-yellow light of dawn began to wake up the colors of the land. A field of dark, round stones near the track suddenly sprouted long necks and legs, as a flock of emus woke and began stretching and preening. They watched curiously as he walked past—he was walking now, and feeling tired, but still not sleepy. In an odd way, he'd never felt so wide awake. The air was clear and fresh; the whole world was spread out at his feet, rolling down towards the desert.

That's when Kokako realized that the baked earth under his feet was warm, and getting warmer. In fact, it was uncomfortably hot, even through the soles of his sandals.

And the rock just ahead wasn't an emu. It wasn't a rock either.

It moved, twisting around to face him. Its surface was black, rough and jagged like hardened lava, with shards of what looked like opal and sharp crystals of red and clear stone here and there. Fine cracks glared the orange and scarlet of molten stone as it bent and turned.

Kokako felt as though the world had dropped away beneath him, leaving him floating in a strange little bubble, where all the sounds were very far away, except for a sort of ringing in his ears. He had to glance down, to see that he had drawn Anna's sword. His hand felt as if it belonged to someone else on the other side of the world.

The rock-man straightened up, rising into a lumpy sort of pillar. It bulged and folded, until it had a distinct, squarish head and a pair of thick arms.

"Right!" said Kokako, and his voice squeaked like a baby mouse's. "Right," he said, more firmly and in his proper voice. "I want some answers." And he pointed the sword at the rock-man.

It flowed along the ground until it was almost touching the tip of the sword. Kokako clenched his teeth and held the blade steady. The rock-man's eyes were two glowing pits of lava. Heat blasted off it as though it were a blacksmith's forge, and Kokako's knees suddenly went weak as he realized what would happen if he had to fight—the sword would be no use at all. Like a smith's forge, the rock-man's body gave off enough heat to soften steel. He could feel his hair and his eyebrows getting frizzy.

"Ask," the rock-man rumbled.

Kokako backed away a few steps, before he realized what it, or he—Kokako had a feeling the rock-man *was* a man, and not a rock-woman—had said. The voice was almost too low to hear. Just as in the *Oyon*-Shrine, he seemed to feel it in his ribs as much as in his ears. There didn't seem to be a mouth.

"Ask?"

"Ask."

"Um ..." He hadn't expected this. "Was it you in the *Oyon*-Shrine?"

"Yes. Ask, twice more."

"Twice—you mean you'll only answer three questions?

That wasn't a question!" Kokako added hastily. "I was just thinking out loud. Three questions, like in fairy tales? And that wasn't a question either."

The glowing eyes narrowed and grew wider again, somehow changing the shape of the rock-man's face. Kokako thought it was a sort of a laugh.

What kind of question would get the answers he needed? He sheathed the sword and stepped off to the grass, still wet with dew, to cool his feet and put a little more distance between them. Did the rock-man want to answer, or did he simply have to answer?

"What were you doing there?" The rock-man couldn't get away with just yes or no to that, even if he wanted to.

The rock-man considered. "Traveling, seeing new lands. Exploring. But am weak, away from home. Lord Barramundi, sorcerer, learned my secret name through magic. Bound me. Cannot resist, must serve him three times, three tasks."

Every word was slow, as if it had to rise from the depths of the earth. Kokako did not for one moment make the mistake of thinking that meant the rock-man was stupid.

"Made a house, deep in rock. That was first task. Sorcerer carries me to … what you call *Oyon*. First we are at salt lake, then we are at *Oyon*-Shrine. Great magic. I caught the …" Again, there was the winking of the fiery eyes. The rock-man thought something he was saying was funny. "Caught the burning *Oyon* in a blanket of utter night. Cold," he added, as though that were important. "Very, very cold, you see, small human. Burning *Oyon* too hot for human flesh to seize. Grows cold in blanket, so sorcerer can take her. That was second task."

"Her? The *Oyon*'s a *girl*? And that wasn't—"

"Yes. Not a question." The rock-man was definitely laughing.

But it had been quite a detailed answer. The rock-man must want him to know as much as possible, Kokako thought.

"Now I go back to sorcerer. Not told to go quickly. Not told to go straight. Seeing more new lands on way." The rock-man sounded very smug about that. He clearly enjoyed annoying his master.

"I suppose you wouldn't tell me your secret name even if I asked you that as my third question," Kokako said hopefully, but being very careful to keep his voice from rising and turning it into a question.

The rock-man said nothing.

"Probably against the rules," Kokako agreed with its silence. "Alright. Let me think."

He wondered, while he was trying to think of the best third question, how the cold opal *Oyon* could be so hot only a rock-man could touch it, and, since the rock-man must be an Old Thing like Torrie, if Torrie had a secret name. If he found it out, would Torrie have to perform three tasks for him?

≈≈≈≈≈

If I had a secret name, I certainly wouldn't tell Kokako what it was, and I'm not telling you, either. You see what happened to the rock-man when someone found out his secret name. That's why they're supposed to be secret. There's power in names, for us Old Things.

∾∾∾∾∾

Kokako took a deep breath. "Alright. I need to find the sorcerer and save the *Oyon*, if it wasn't destroyed and can be saved. What help can you give me?" There, that was fairly clear. So long as the rock-man didn't say, "None."

But he just stood as though deep in thought, with the air dancing in a heat-haze over him.

"One who might help," he said at last. "Give you advice, maybe. Send you to that one. Sorcerer didn't tell me not to."

Definitely a sort of grin, the way his face tilted and fine cracks spread around the eyes. Kokako grinned back.

"Where do I find this person?" he asked. That couldn't count as an extra question, because obviously the rock-man would have to give him directions.

The rock-man didn't answer. He merely turned his head and made some odd, windy rumbling noises.

Kokako frowned, listening, but he couldn't hear any words in it.

Then there was a pattering in the grass, and he felt something moving behind him. He jumped and looked over his shoulder. There was a big emu, almost as tall as a man, looking down at him with shiny dark eyes, and the rest of the flock, a dozen of them, were loping up, necks outstretched.

Kokako stood his ground, but he felt a little flutter of fear in his stomach. They might only eat grass and fruit and bugs, but they were certainly all far bigger than him.

"Ride," the rock-man said. "My friends help. Sorcerer is dangerous to all."

The biggest of the emus sidled up to Kokako, tilting its head first one way, then the other. It opened and shut its beak a few times, nervously. Kokako felt about as nervous.

"Going now," the rock-man said, as if that was that, and he swung around and went flowing away, burning a new strip in the yellow grass. Just as in the *Oyon*-Shrine, he moved far faster than Kokako could run. The rock-man headed up a ridge, onto hard mountain stone where he left no track at all, and soon he was lost to sight, one dark rock among many. Kokako suspected the rock-man had known he was being followed, and had actually wanted someone to catch up. He wondered if there was some way to free the Old Thing from the sorcerer who had his secret name. Maybe Torrie would know …

The emu pecked Kokako's shoulder impatiently, then squatted down as if it were brooding over a nest of eggs.

"Ride?" Kokako said helplessly. "Are you sure?"

The only answer was an impatient shove from another emu's beak. Carefully, he swung a leg over the squatting bird's back, sitting down with his knees hooked in front of its stubby little wings. It was very soft, like a warm cushion, and its dark feathers were more like silky hair. There wasn't anything to hold on to, but he'd ridden a donkey often enough when he lived with his grandmother to know that you didn't hold on with your hands anyway, but with your legs and your sense of

balance. Which didn't mean he wouldn't have liked something to hold on to.

The emu, with a sort of disapproving churking noise, bounded up, and the whole flock set off, heading west in long strides.

"Wait, wait!" Kokako cried. "We should wait for my friends; they won't know what happened to me!"

But either the emus didn't care, or they didn't understand human speech. They kept on running, and all Kokako could do was sit tight and try not to fall.

I wasn't too worried, at first, when I woke up and found Kokako gone. His blankets were still in a heap by the fire, and his pack was still piled with ours. Jix, too, remained, perched sleeping on Anna's boots.

"Hey!" I shouted, "Kokako? Breakfast!"

There was no answering shout. Jix didn't stir, but Anna sat up, yawning and rubbing her eyes. "What's wrong?" she asked, and then, "Where's my sword?"

"Kokako," I said, which answered both questions.

"He's probably gone off to practice his sword-drill," Anna said, looking around. "He won't have gone far."

The problem was, there was such a good view from where we were that if he hadn't gone far, we should have been able to see him.

"Still," I said crossly, "wandering around alone in mountains is never a good idea, if you're a boy from the city, no matter how much you might have learned out of books."

Anna gave me a look. "Right," she said. She picked up her boots and shook the parrot off. He woke up and tumbled into the air, turning right side up with a startled squawk.

"Where's Kokako?" Anna demanded, as she hopped on one foot, pulling a boot on the other. "Ask him, Torrie."

"Where did Kokako go?" I asked.

"Who? What?" Jix flapped heavily to my shoulder. "Where?"

"Wake up!" I said crossly. "Kokako's gone. Where did he go, and why did he take Anna's sword?"

"How should I know?" Jix said. "Where's breakfast?"

"Go find your own, and look for Kokako while you're at it!"

While we waited for Jix to come back, we ate leftover pancakes for breakfast, but didn't bother about a fire and tea. I made sure Anna did eat, though. No matter how worried you are, you can't go clambering up and down mountainsides on an empty stomach, and I was beginning to be afraid we might have to do some clambering. If he'd gone off to practice, and gotten lost or fallen into a ravine …

Anna started pacing and biting her braid.

I climbed up onto a high outcropping of rock and looked around. I couldn't see any sign of Kokako. After a while I did spot a rainbow flash of color, and Jix came swooping down.

"I can't see him anywhere," the parrot said, landing on my shoulder and burying his face in my fur. "Nowhere. I even went and asked those rude budgies down in the ravine, and they hadn't seen him. But he'll be alright, won't he? There aren't any crocodiles up here."

"Of course there are no crocodiles up here," I said, with a heavy feeling in my stomach. "Anna …"

She could tell by my face that it wasn't good news.

"We'd better search for him ourselves," she said.

We did.

We found the footprints of sandals in what we thought was the rock-man's ashy trail, so we packed up and left the road to follow it, up and over the saddle of land, with all the west before us, as the mountains dropped away towards the grassy highlands and the distant desert.

After about nine miles or so, the footprints disappeared. Maybe Kokako had started walking on the grass instead, but there were no marks of human prints in the rapidly drying dew, only scuffling long strides that I could hardly believe in—they looked like the tracks of giant birds.

"Um ..." I said. "I don't know how to say this, but the only tracks I can see now look like they were left by giant birds."

"Probably emus," said Jix.

"Emus?" I repeated, and looked at Anna, to see if she knew anything about them.

"Big birds," Anna said. "You could feed *Shrike*'s whole crew breakfast with just one egg." She considered. "Well, maybe two or three. Mister Flytch and Banksy can eat an awful lot of breakfast."

So everybody knew about emus except me. "Do these emus eat humans?" I asked.

Anna laughed. "Not that I know of."

That was some comfort. But none the less, Kokako had disappeared and now there was nothing for me to track.

We couldn't even follow the track of the rock-creature. Not far from where we lost Kokako, its trail disappeared among the stones. Jix flew over, searching for Kokako, and Anna and I spent an entire day climbing and calling among the rocks, but we found no trace of him.

Finally, we had no choice. We decided to go on. We both thought that whatever had become of Kokako, he would be heading for the desert. If we kept on, we might find some clue.

"Kokako's not dead, is he?" Jix asked miserably, when we made that decision.

"No," I said firmly. If he were dead, we should have found

some trace, some bones or clothes, if something had eaten him. And I couldn't believe the rock-man would have burned him up, although I kept being afraid in the back of my mind. But I had to reassure Jix. We didn't need a panicked parrot on our hands.

"He's just … misplaced. Lost. We'll find him, don't worry."

"I'm not worrying."

But we all were, of course.

≈≈≈≈≈

Anna, Jix, and I went on searching for any sign that Kokako had gone that way, as we headed down the long, gradual western slopes of the mountains, into the Bookabee Highlands, where the grass was yellowish and dry, prickly and rasping and rustling, and red kangaroos lolloped slowly along, browsing as they went, or bounded in great leaps. At night, stocky black wombats peered out of their burrows and bustled about nibbling away, rather like rabbits. Human farms were scattered through the highlands, and sheep grazed, watching us with wary yellow eyes.

I asked the sheep (who really weren't much use, being very woolly minded) and the kangaroos and the wombats, of course, and Anna asked the few humans we saw, but nobody had seen a boy on his own. It was as though the wind had carried him away.

CHAPTER SEVEN

# Which is very windy

K okako traveled with the emus for several days. Every morning they spread out over the grassy hills, grazing and chasing grasshoppers, leaving Kokako alone, hungry, tired, and hot. During the nights, they all hunched down on the ground together, with Kokako in the middle. He picked raspberries in the tangles of brush alongside the riverbeds, kept his water gourd filled, and tried a few wild plums, but they weren't ripe yet and made his insides feel peculiar.

On the second day, when he felt faint and sick from hunger, he used Anna's sword to dig up some plants with flowers like little yellow daisies or dandelions, which were growing in the dappled shade of a grove of trees along yet another dried-up stream. He was almost certain the plants were a root vegetable called a yam daisy, so he rubbed the mud off and ate one. It didn't taste bad, and it didn't make him feel any sicker, so he decided the plant was safe and dug up a bunch, tying them to his belt, in case there weren't any later.

He wondered how long he could live, eating raw yam daisy roots and raspberries. He wondered if the emus were really taking him someplace, or if, being bird-brains, they'd forgotten all about whatever it was the rock-man had told them. Maybe they'd forgotten he wasn't an emu. Maybe they were going to keep him forever. He'd heard of children growing up wild, adopted by kangaroos or dingos, but to be adopted by emus seemed a bit … silly.

Once he saw a flock of sheep grazing in the distance and decided to find the farmers and ask for help, but when he started to walk away, the emus all came charging after him, nudging him back to where they had been grazing. No escape. The biggest one crouched down for him to get on and they were off.

Kokako had no idea where the road was anymore. He knew Anna and Torrie were never going to be able to catch up. They might still be in the mountains looking for him. They might think he was dead. When he started feeling like that, he distracted himself by writing, in his head, long sections of his book, all about the grassy highlands and the emus. *For the emu, the humble blue grasshopper is a tasty treat …* It was too easy to fall into a swamp of misery, otherwise.

The hills grew flatter and flatter and drier and drier, and one morning Kokako woke up to a strange smell on the wind. It was hot and dusty—the desert.

The waterhole they came to early that morning had only a little water in the bottom of it. Kokako drank deeply and ate the last of the yam daisies. When he turned his back on the distant mountains, the land stretched out before him, red, dotted with clumps of twisted little bushes or tussocks of rattling yellow grass. The horizon was hazy, red fading up into brownish and then the blue of the sky above. It looked almost like a sunset, but since it was morning and the sun was behind him, he knew it wasn't. He shaded his eyes and stared at it. The redness was rising higher, and the wind blew hot and stinging into his face.

The emus milled around him, touching him with their beaks.

"What?" he asked. "I don't understand what you want."

This time, they didn't seem to want anything. They weren't pushing or poking at him, just—saying good-bye, he realized, as first one and then another turned away, stalking through the grass, snapping at grasshoppers, and, all at once, breaking into a run.

"Hey!" Kokako shouted. "You can't just leave me here!" There was no point running after them; he didn't have the energy, and anyway, he'd never catch up to an emu. They were already almost out of sight, a bobbing gray mass disappearing into the distance.

High overhead, a black eagle circled. Probably it would come down to pick his bones once he was dead, Kokako thought, blinking at the prickling behind his eyelids. He must have gotten some sand in his eyes.

The eagle was spiraling lower. It passed over him with a whoosh of feathers and came back for a second look.

"Go away!" Kokako shouted. "I'm not dead yet!"

The eagle gave a loud cry, as though it were laughing at him.

Kokako sat down by the waterhole to think. There were emu tracks in the mud, and dingo tracks, and the paw marks of big kangaroos. Some of his own sandal tracks, too, but trampled all over by emus and hardly visible. There were no sheep tracks, so he couldn't follow a sheep path and hope to find human help. Probably the best thing to do would be to turn around and head back towards the mountains, hoping to meet Anna and Torrie looking for him, hoping he wasn't found first by a pack of hungry dingoes.

The wind flung sand in his face. When he looked out towards the desert, the red haze had turned to a cloud, dust boiling up off the land and spinning, whirling.

A whirlwind. Kokako turned to run for a distant clump of yellow-flowered wattle bushes for shelter, but the eagle was there on the ground, hissing at him, spreading its wings.

The wind screamed with voices, shrill shrieks and deep roaring, and he tried to dodge the eagle, but it bounded into the air and flew at him. He ducked, covering his head with his hands, and the winds grabbed him, tugging and dragging him towards the desert. It felt as though there were about a dozen clawed hands digging into him. He was deafened by the shrieking, which almost seemed to have words in it. He saw the eagle give a little bobbing bow of its head before taking flight, soaring away, avoiding the wildest air currents. His feet were no longer on the ground. He was tumbling in the air, drowning in a dry red sea of choking dust. Sand pounded him, piercing his skin like a thousand needles. With his last sensible thought, Kokako pulled a fold of his cape over his head, and after that, there was only noise, and heat, and darkness.

≈≈≈≈≈

"I heard there was an eagle looking for a human boy," a fat young wombat told me, sitting back on his haunches. "A wren told me she heard from a parrot who heard from a kite that there was an eagle hanging around the edge of the desert. Waiting for a boy to show up. And you know what those eagles are like." The wombat paused, chewing busily.

"No," I said. "I don't, actually."

"Well," said the wombat. "They hang around with the Wind Dancers. And I heard there was a big whirlwind, only a couple of days ago. Eagles can summon Wind Dancers, they say. Is that a puffball, over there?"

"I think so," I said. The wombat waddled over to the puffball on his short little legs, his great bulky body jiggling as though he were wearing a suit that was too large. "What are Wind Dancers?"

The wombat stared at me, his eyes like black buttons in the moonlight. "You're an Old Thing, and you don't know Wind Dancers?" he asked, his mouth full of puffball.

"I'm from away," I reminded him.

"Wind Dancers are Old Things from the heart of the deserts. They live in the desert winds. Maybe they *are* the desert winds." The wombat was almost whispering now. "Although they can travel far from the desert, too. People say you never see them, but you hear their voices in the storm."

"Are they dangerous?" I asked.

"You've never seen a whirlwind, or a desert thunderstorm, have you?" the wombat retorted. "Of course they're dangerous."

"I wonder why they'd want Kokako?" I was thinking out loud, but the wombat gave a shrug.

"I certainly don't know. Excuse me, Torrie, do you mind? I think that's a yam daisy you're sitting on."

I thanked the wombat and headed back to the campfire, where Anna was sitting with a morose Jix on her shoulder.

"Any luck?" she asked, without much hope in her voice.

"Yes," I said. "At last. But I don't think it's good news."

I told her what I had learned from the wombat.

"So Kokako did make it this far," she said.

"Maybe," I agreed cautiously. "I did think I saw his footprints back on the edge of a stream, two days ago, but there were so many sheep and kangaroo tracks it was hard to tell."

Anna fidgeted with her braid. "So there was an eagle looking for him, for these Wind Dancers. I don't like the sound of that. Since the sorcerer has sand-goblins and one of the rock-folk working for him, he's probably got other Old Things on his side, too."

"At least we can be fairly certain we didn't abandon Kokako in the mountains," I pointed out, trying to look on the bright side. "And we know he isn't dead."

"I should have stayed in Keastipol," said Anna. "Kokako

would have been safer if we'd taken him to sea with us."

"It was his decision to make. Not yours. It's not your fault he disappeared."

Anna nodded, but I could tell that didn't make her feel a lot better.

"I'll go look for eagles in the morning," Jix told me, his voice a bit unsteady.

"That's rather brave of you," I said.

Jix ruffled his feathers a little, and hunched his head between his shoulders. I think we both suspected eagles might eat parrots, when they had a chance.

In the morning Jix took to the air, nervously looking for eagles, and Anna and I left the last of the grassy highlands behind us.

The desert stretched ahead, already shimmering with heat. The few scrubby little trees cast purple shadows in the dawn light. We turned towards a dark line of trees, tall gums that fol-

lowed a dry, cracked riverbed. Perhaps when the Wind Dancers called up a thunderstorm it would fill with rain, flowing out into the desert to be sucked down into the red earth.

"We'll follow this," Anna decided. "We'll be more likely to find waterholes along the river's course, and it'll be easier to walk in the shade. And at the waterholes, there are bound to be animals or even Old Things you can ask about Kokako, Torrie."

I agreed. We certainly couldn't strike out across the desert with no idea where we were going or where the next water might be.

I picked up a few seeds under the trees and handed them to Anna.

"It's not as much fun without Kokako," she said.

"We'll find him." I was reassuring myself as much as her. "Look, Jix is coming back in an awful hurry."

"Is anything chasing him?" Anna picked up a stone to throw, but Jix was alone. He landed panting on top of my head, and I uncorked my water gourd and dribbled some into the palm of my hand so he could drink.

"The eagle," he said then, still panting. "Chased me. But I asked her anyway. She said the rock-man sent Kokako to the desert." Jix dipped up another beakful of water, and I told Anna what he had said.

"To where in the desert?" she demanded.

"To the camp at the red rock towers on the Sleeping River," Jix said. "To the human there."

Anna and I looked at one another.

"The sorcerer," said Anna grimly.

# CHAPTER EIGHT

# In which Kokako meets a stranger

Kokako woke up with a strange feeling in his head. When he sat up, sand dribbled out of his hair and ran down his face. He shook himself, like Jix waking up. Dust flew everywhere. He felt bruised and battered and every place his clothes touched him hurt, as though his skin were scraped from sliding on a rough rug.

Sand, he remembered. Whirling dust. The whirlwind. No wonder he hurt. The wonder was that he was alive.

That strange feeling in his head was echoing silence.

"Hello?" he croaked. No one answered, but at least he could hear his own voice, so he hadn't been permanently deafened.

Feeling a bit shaky, Kokako got to his feet. He had been lying on a striped blanket on a stony floor, covered with his cape. His water gourd and Anna's sword were both lying on the floor. He fastened them to his belt again and set out to explore. It was quite dark, but away in the distance, up a sloping, uneven floor, there was blinding white light—daylight. Cool rock walls leaned in over him, making a high triangular space. The air smelled damp. Kokako turned his back on the light and followed the smell of water to where the cave grew narrower, climbing over shallow shelves of rock, trying not to stub his toes. There was still a little light coming from a long crack overhead, where the inward-leaning walls of the cave didn't quite meet. Near the end he could touch them with a hand out on either side. But tight spaces didn't bother him, and anyway, the thin shaft of light from above glinted on shiny darkness. *Water.* A slick shimmer showed where a spring was seeping down from cracks in the wall to form a pool.

Kokako drank and drank, and washed himself where a trickle of water flowed out from the pool, losing itself amid the uneven shelves of rock on the cave floor. Then he headed back up towards the cave mouth.

A little beyond where he had been sleeping, he found another neat bed of blankets and a leather pack a little like Anna's. For a moment he thought it was hers, but then he realized it couldn't be. There was a bow and a quiver of arrows lying beside it, which didn't belong to Anna, and besides, Anna wouldn't have left him to wake up alone and confused, she'd have been sitting right there by him. He hesitated, then drew the sword before he went on.

At the mouth of the cave there was a small fire burning, and a teakettle just coming to the boil. A covered frying pan sat on a stone, flatbread was baking on another, and the smell of food made his mouth water.

"Hello?" he tried again.

There was a thump, and a tall woman dropped down from the outcropping overhead, landing lightly on her toes in front of him. Kokako yelled and jumped backwards, raising the sword to guard the way Anna had taught him.

The woman looked him over, dusting grit off her hands. Then she took a pair of eyeglasses out of her pocket, put them on, and looked him over again. "Oh, yes," she said. "You're the boy the Wind Dancers dropped into my camp. Very peculiar. What on earth do they expect me to do with you?"

"Um," said Kokako, lowering the sword. "I'm Kokako. A rock-man sent me," he added hopefully. "And some emus. They thought you could help."

"Really? I don't know any rock-folk," the woman said. "Or emus. No, I definitely don't know any emus. Have you had your breakfast?"

"Um, no."

"Well, it's too late for breakfast, anyway."

Kokako felt his hollow, aching stomach shrink in on itself even more. His legs felt as if they weren't quite connected to his body.

"You certainly look like you need something." The woman pushed her glasses up a bit higher on her nose. "You can call it breakfast anyhow, if you like."

"Yes, *please*."

"Sit down, then."

Kokako sat, and watched the woman as she peeled a big

circle of flatbread off the rock. She scraped a mess of chopped meat and vegetables in thick yellow sauce out of the frying pan, rolled it all up in the bread, and handed it to him. Kokako didn't worry about what kind of meat it was, although he rather hoped it wasn't emu, at least, not any emus he knew. He devoured it in huge mouthfuls, despite the fact that it was horribly hot with foreign spices and made his eyes water.

The woman watched him with a little smile, as if she liked the way he ate her cooking. She handed him a mug of tea, and

watched him drink that, too. The way she watched him made Kokako feel a bit like a scientist's specimen in a cage, so he figured it was fair to study her right back.

She wasn't from the Great Southern Continent, but she didn't look like she was from Anna's part of the world, either. She had brown skin that was lighter than his and darker than Anna's, and wore a cotton scarf that had once been white, but was now mostly dust-colored, twisted loosely around her head to make a turban. The ends of her short black hair stuck out in spikes beneath it. Her eyes were a pale green, and she had gold rings in her ears and a blue sapphire in the side of her nose. She was wearing a white tunic, which like her scarf was mostly the reddish color of the desert, but instead of sandals she wore sturdy boots. There was something strangely familiar about her, too. He couldn't think what it was.

Kokako finished his tea. "Thank you," he said, feeling a bit shy now. "I haven't eaten much at all in days."

The woman wasn't listening. She was rummaging in the satchel that hung from her heavy belt. After a moment she pulled out a battered, water-stained, leather-bound notebook and a pencil. "Tell me about the Wind Dancers," she commanded. "Tell me everything. More tea?"

It was not a pleasant journey, the one Anna and I made into the Dandarigan Desert. It was hotter than either of us had ever imagined being. The sun burned down, and the heat struck up from the ground with a savage force. The distance wavered as though we were looking through water, but it was only waves of heat rippling the air. Anna's clothes were soaked with sweat from the time we set out in the morning until the sun set, and of course losing all that moisture made her even thirstier. I sometimes wondered how anyone could stand to live out there. Jix was a forest parrot and he couldn't fly much in the heat; he rode on Anna's shoulder or on mine, his beak gaping a little, panting.

At night, it cooled off so quickly we were left shivering with cold, huddled back to back by the fire under all our blankets. We followed the sunken dry watercourse we hoped was the eagle's Sleeping River. Most days, we managed to find a muddy waterhole somewhere along the way. As Anna had suggested, these were good places for me to ask questions, since all the desert animals came to them to drink.

For some reason, everyone always turned shy and made excuses to leave, when I asked about the sorcerer. But one morning a kangaroo did tell me that there was in fact a place, another two days' journey along the river, where great red outcroppings of rock rose like towers from the desert. That gave us the heart to go on, no matter how hot it was, or how thirsty and weary we felt. The kangaroo also gave me some advice.

"Don't sleep in the riverbed," he said. "If there's a storm up in the Bookabee Highlands, the Sleeping River will wake up and come roaring down until the desert swallows it. You don't want to be in its path, if that happens."

I'd already had a similar thought myself. It sounded like

good advice, even if it was hard to picture this dry, sunken roadway as a raging torrent of water; we were careful always to sleep a little distance from the river's bed.

The desert was not pleasant, and yet, there was an incredible beauty in it. The mountains fell behind us, pale blues and pinks, and the red land stretched out in all directions, speckled with stands of dark bushes and prickly yellow grass. The air was dry and clean, and the sky went on forever, a clear, pure, cloudless blue.

"It reminds me of the ocean," Anna said the next afternoon, as we walked along a stretch where there was not a single shadow at all to give us shade. "You feel you have space to be yourself, out here. I can see why Kokako dreams of exploring it."

"I've never had any problem being myself anywhere," I said.

Maybe I sounded a bit cross. I'm not a creature that likes the heat. Anna had a white scarf wrapped around her head to keep it a little cooler, and she'd rolled up her sleeves and the legs of her trousers. I didn't have anything to take off or roll up, unless I decided to shave myself, and then I'd probably get a sunburn. Despite her scarf and her tan, Anna's face was red and peeling.

"That's because you're an Old Thing, Torrie," Anna said. "Humans are always wondering about themselves, wondering what they really are. It's part of what makes us do things, stretch ourselves. Go off on adventures."

"I just adventure for the fun of it," I said. "Which right now seems rather foolish."

"That's why—look!" Anna pointed into the distance. "Do you suppose those are the red rock towers?"

She dug out her telescope, and I shaded my eyes, peering into the afternoon glare.

The things we were looking at weren't towers built by anyone except the forces of the earth. They were big outcroppings of red sandstone, the layers weathered and worn so that they looked like stacks of plates. When Anna passed me the telescope, I could see a dark, triangular opening between two touching stone stacks. As I watched, something moved, climbing down from the top of the highest outcropping, a small, thin figure in a dusty tunic that might once have been white.

"Kokako!" I shouted. "He's climbing on the rocks."

"Kokako!" shrieked Jix, and took off in a flurry of feathers.

"No! Wait!" I shouted after the parrot. "Remember the sorcerer!"

But Jix was gone.

"Let's go," said Anna. "Look, there's more river gums along belong the rock towers, and the bed of the river itself is worn quite low. If we keep in under shelter, we should be able to sneak up close without being seen. Then you can go and scout around invisibly, and I'll be close enough to help if you need me."

I nodded. It sounded like a good plan, but I wished Anna had her sword.

"Watch out for goblins," I reminded her.

Anna patted the knife in her belt. "Don't worry about me."

We crept along the undercut bank, right against the reaching roots of the trees. There was quite a large pool of water beneath them, almost enough to make the river look like a river. It wasn't salty, though. I tasted it, to find out. A flock of bright green budgies took off, rising up into the sky like a cloud of shrieking green steam.

"So much for sneaking," Anna said.

"I'll go find Kokako." I hopped up onto the bank, spear in hand, invisible to everyone, even Kokako, since I didn't want him to make some startled sound and alert his guards, if he had any. I had barely started to sneak towards the rocks when I heard Kokako shouting.

"Torrie? Anna? Are you there?"

Jix had found him, and of course, he knew we must be close, too. I gave up on being invisible, and Anna climbed up into sight as Kokako came running with Jix clinging to his shoulder.

"There you are!" he said happily. "I knew you'd find a way to follow me."

"You're lucky we found you," Anna said severely. "Didn't you think how worried we'd be, when you went off alone like that? We were afraid you were dead!"

Kokako, after one look at her, bit his lip. "I didn't mean to," he said. "I'm sorry—about taking your sword and not coming back and everything. I thought I'd be back in an hour or so. And I told Jix, so you wouldn't worry."

"Jix didn't ..." Anna and I both glowered at the parrot, who ducked his head and scratched it with his foot, looking as embarrassed as it's possible for a parrot to look.

"Jix …" I said sternly.

"He didn't. He might have. I don't remember!" the bird muttered into his feathers. "I was asleep."

Kokako unbuckled the sword from his belt and held it out. "It was the rock-man, he said he'd send me to someone who could give us advice about finding the *Oyon,* and the emus wouldn't listen when I said I wanted to wait for you, and she said she didn't have any way to send you a message …"

"Who said?" I asked.

But Anna was staring beyond Kokako, towards the red rocks and the woman coming out of the shadows. She put her hand on my head to steady herself, as if she suddenly felt weak in the knees.

"*Mother?*" she said.

"Ah, there you are, Anna," said Annapurna Khanum, as if meeting a daughter you haven't seen for a couple of years, in the middle of the desert in the middle of the Great Southern Continent, were perfectly ordinary. "I don't suppose you've seen any Wind Dancers? Kokako wasn't able to give me a very good description."

"But I couldn't help it," said Kokako seriously. "It was just all whirling sand."

Anna made a noise halfway between a laugh and an exasperated sigh. "Of *course* she's here in the middle of the desert," she muttered to me. "I should have been expecting it, since I knew she was on the Great Southern Continent. Why am I even surprised?" And she went to throw her arms around her mother in a hug.

"You're supposed to say, *My goodness, Anna, you've grown, and I'm so sorry I forgot to come home for so long*," Anna said to her. Her words might have sounded carefully light and joking, but her grip on her mother was tight, and her voice shook a little. I suppose if she didn't joke, she would have had to either cry or shout, and neither would have done any good.

"But I didn't forget," Annapurna said. "I had to write another book, so that I could afford to make an expedition into the desert. I wrote a letter to say so, asking your father to sail down here to stay with me. Didn't you get it?"

"No."

"Oh. I thought I'd sent it. No wonder the two of you never came. I wonder what I did with it?"

"Probably wrote part of your book on it," Anna said.

Annapurna Khanum laughed ruefully, looking just the slightest bit embarrassed. "I suppose I might have. Anyway, you're here now. Is your father with you?"

I began to see why Anna found her mother so exasperating. She was one of those people who drifts along in a world of her own, always very surprised when her little bubble bumps up against other people's needs and problems. It seemed to me, watching Anna, that she, and probably her father too, had long ago decided there was no point getting angry at Annapurna or trying to change her. It was the way she was, and because they loved her, they accepted that their family was mostly just the two of them. Annapurna would wander back from time to time, like a ship returning to its home port, only to leave again on another voyage. Perhaps, being sailors themselves, they found it easier to understand her restless need to travel.

"I'm captain of my own ship now," Anna said. "And did you even know Father was captured by the pirate-queen?"

I tugged at Kokako's tunic. "Come on," I said. "We should go put the kettle on for tea. Or something."

"It's not really time for tea," Kokako started to say, and then he said, "Oh, yes, right. That's a good idea."

So we went off to the cave to make tea, and left the two of them alone for a little.

When they came to join us, they were both looking a little teary, but happy, so I guess everything was all right between them. Humans are strange and complicated things, that's all I can say.

"But what are you doing here, Mother?" Anna asked, as they sat down and Kokako handed them each a tin mug of tea.

"She's exploring," Kokako said eagerly. "She's going to write about the edge of the desert and the Bookabee Highlands in her next book, aren't you?"

"Well, yes," Annapurna Khanum admitted, scratching her head under her turban. "Although, actually ..."

"Actually what?" Anna asked.

"Actually, I heard from *my* mother a little while ago. Since I was already here on the Great Southern Continent, she wanted me to be, um, a sort of a spy. But *mostly*, I'm writing a book about the desert-edge."

"But—you're not an enemy," said Kokako. "Why would you want to spy on us?"

"A spy for whom?" I asked, which seemed to me the most sensible question.

"Spying on what?" Anna asked. "There's not a lot out here in the desert to spy on."

Annapurna Khanum grinned, and for a moment she looked a lot like Anna. "It's my Wicked Uncle again," she said. "Your grandmother knew he had come here, and when she found out I had, too, she wanted me to find out what he was up to this time, and let her know."

"The Wicked Uncle …" Anna said.

"Wait a minute," I said.

"Oh, no." Anna held her head in both hands, as if she thought it might be about to fall off. "Not—Lord Barramundi. The sorcerer Kokako's looking for."

"Well, that's not his real name, of course," Annapurna Khanum said. "I don't actually know what his real name is. They're very secretive about that sort of thing, in my mother's family."

"No, no, no!" said Anna. "Why didn't you ever tell me you were related to sorcerers?"

Annapurna blinked. "It never seemed very important before. And my uncle shouldn't be your problem."

"Well, he is now," Anna said grimly. "Kokako's being blamed for destroying the *Oyon,* and it was Lord Barramundi who stole it."

I could see she was thinking that she had just finished sorting out a problem her pirate grandfather had caused, and now, here she was in the middle of another mess caused by her family.

"People can't help who their relatives are," I said comfortingly, and patted her hand.

Kokako wasn't worrying about that. "But if you've been spying on Lord Barramundi, Annapurna," he said eagerly, "you can help us, like the rock-man said."

Annapurna frowned thoughtfully. "I don't see how. *I'm* not a sorcerer. But my mother is, you see, and she's had a lot of practice, keeping Uncle from causing trouble. I'll send her a letter, once I get to a port—"

"If you remember," Anna interrupted, a little rudely, but Annapurna just laughed.

"No!" said Kokako, surprising us all by contradicting his

hero. "You can't! I mean, we can't wait that long. There's going to be a war, if we don't do something soon. The other cities are going to attack Keastipol! They might already be fighting! We have to get the *Oyon* back *now,* not wait months and months while you send letters …" He trailed off, looking embarrassed and upset. "We have to stop them fighting," he whispered.

"Kokako's right," Anna said. "We came out here to help him get the *Oyon* back and clear his name, and that's what we're going to do."

"We can do more than that," I said. They all looked at me. I coughed importantly. "We already know they won't listen to Kokako, and Anna's just a foreign sea captain. But Annapurna Khanum is famous. If she goes to Keastipol and tells the magistrates that while she was in the desert she met a sorcerer who had the *Oyon* …"

"I didn't actually *meet* him," Annapurna Khanum said. "I only found out where he was. He doesn't like me, and I don't like goblins."

"Sh!" I said, as authoritatively as a magistrate myself. "Let me finish. The cities might listen to her. She might be able to persuade them there actually was a sorcerer, and prevent them fighting. And we'd have time to find the *Oyon* and get it back."

"Yes!" Kokako said.

Anna nodded slowly. "It's a good idea," she said.

Annapurna Khanum scratched the tip of her earlobe thoughtfully. "I don't know," she said. "Those magistrates can be pretty bull-headed. If they've decided Kokako destroyed the *Oyon,* or that another city stole it, they're not going to want to change their minds. People like that often think that changing their minds makes them look weak, or foolish. They'd rather be wrong and keep insisting they're not, than admit they made a mistake."

"But you have to try," Kokako pleaded. "Please, Annapurna. I try not to think about it, but it's always there in the back of my mind—people fighting, houses burning—like the carvings on the *Oyon*-Shrine showing what it was like before Tero Korax the Wanderer came. Please try."

"But …" said Annapurna Khanum, with a look at Anna. No matter how irresponsible she was towards her family, I guess she didn't want to leave her daughter again so soon.

"It's the best plan," Anna said. "You know it is, Mother. You head for Keastipol and try to persuade the magistrates there truly is a sorcerer behind it all. And we'll get the *Oyon*." She took a deep breath. "And you wait for me in Keastipol, wait on the *Shrike*. Don't get distracted and wander off somewhere else. Promise?"

"I promise," Annapurna Khanum said meekly. Then she laughed and Anna laughed and shook her head.

"One thing you're all forgetting," I pointed out, "is that no matter who he's related to, we still don't know where to find Lord Barramundi."

"At the salt lake," said Kokako.

"Yes," I said patiently. "But where's that?"

"Oh, that's easy," Annapurna said. "There are salt lakes all over the desert, but you mean Arcaringa Salt Lake, north of here. I'll draw you a map."

We could see Kokako's face light up. A map, drawn by his hero. Anna and I looked at one another and smiled. We knew who was going to end up looking after that map. We'd be lucky if he didn't sleep with it under his pillow. Well, except that we didn't have any pillows with us.

# CHAPTER NINE

# Which is about the salt lake, sand-goblins, and Wind Dancers

We spent most of the afternoon swimming in the deep pool that was all that was left of the Sleeping River's water, while Annapurna, digging out a little tin paint-box from her pack, sat humming tunelessly atop the highest of the rock towers, with her glasses sliding down her nose, making a map to show us the way to Arcaringa Salt Lake. As afternoon turned into evening we climbed up to join her and sat watching the sun set, letting our hair, or in my case fur, dry in the breeze. Anna, who was combing the knots out of her hair, stopped, frowning at the comb. "You know, I think there's something alive caught in my hair."

"Brine shrimp," said Kokako, after taking a look.

"Yuck."

"If you save them, we can make soup," I pointed out.

Anna gave me a look, and threw the tiny wriggling brine

shrimp over the side of the rock. Some of them might have landed back in the pool.

Anna's mother waved the map in the air to dry the last brushstroke and handed it to Kokako. He accepted it carefully, as though it were some ancient, precious thing that might crumble into dust. Anna and I peered over his shoulders, Anna still dragging a comb through her tangles.

"It's more like a picture than any chart I've seen," Anna commented.

"That's because it's not a sea chart," said her mother. "You don't need to know how many miles away anything is. All you need to know, out here, is where and when you'll find water again."

The map certainly didn't look much like any of Anna's nautical charts. It was painted on papyrus paper in watercolors and had no scale of distances, no compass rose, which is a sort of star showing which way north is on the map, and no lines showing latitude, which is how far you are from the equator. What the map did have was a brown dotted line we were obviously meant to follow. It started at the stone towers on the Sleeping River and headed north, or at least, towards the top, which is usually north on a map. And there was a yellow sun painted on the right, and a red one on the left, which I took to show dawn and dusk, or east and west. The line wiggled back and forth between lumps of rock, all carefully drawn so we'd recognize them when we saw them looming up from the dusty red earth, and careful blue splotches, which were waterholes or wells—the trail zigged and zagged between them. Often there was a little red flame painted by the waterholes, but sometimes the red flames were on their own. Near the top was a large irregular outline, and inside it was painted, *Arcaringa Salt Lake*, in even, old-fashioned letters.

"Those fires must be places to camp," Anna said, her words a bit muffled since she was holding a strip of leather in her mouth while she braided her mostly shrimp-free hair.

"Right," said her mother.

Anna used the thong to tie off the end of the plait and said more clearly, "That must mean we're supposed to make five camps and get there the sixth day?"

Kokako was still looking at the map. "And we'll know which days we need to be especially careful with our water because there won't be a waterhole," he said, and beamed proudly when Annapurna said, "That's right."

"Anna?"

Anna looked up. Her mother, for the first time since I'd met her, looked worried. "Do be careful. He has a whole goblin clan serving him."

Anna dropped a last shrimp (which I ate), and leaned over to give her mother a quick hug. "I got into the pirate-queen's palace and rescued my father. I guess I can probably get into Lord Barramundi's goblin den."

"Ahem."

"*Torrie* and I got into the pirate-queen's palace …"

❧❧❧❧❧

Well rested and feeling almost as though our day at the stone towers had been a holiday, we all set off early the next morning, while the air was still cool and the eastern sky lemon yellow and rosy pink. Kokako and I waited a little distance away, while Anna and her mother said their good-byes. No matter how used they were to being apart, it must have been hard for them to separate after seeing each other only so briefly. But I suppose they were a nautical family, always sailing off hither and yon. And this time, at least, they knew they'd be seeing one another again soon. Unless we were all eaten by goblins or something, of course.

We watched Annapurna Khanum set off, with her heavy pack on her back and her bow slung over her shoulder, striding along the dry bed of the Sleeping River, towards the Bookabee Highlands and eventually, Keastipol. We set off too, leaving the river behind to head towards the north. Anna was very silent for the first mile or so.

"Sorcerers aren't as bad as dragons," I said, and squeezed her hand. I'm not sure if she found that a comforting thought or not, since I don't believe it was actually the sorcerer she was feeling glum about, but she cheered up, and started to whistle.

As the day went on and the sun rose higher, the desert glared and burned, and no one had any energy for whistling. There was rarely any shade. We spent the worst part of each day stretched panting in the few shadows we could find. But the map was good. By keeping a keen eye out for the ridges and rocky outcroppings, we kept ourselves on the path Annapurna Khanum had painted, and exactly where she had shown, there was always a small, mud-edged waterhole at the bottom of some pit, or a crack in the rock we could squeeze through, down into a deep cavern with a pool of water. On five cold desert nights, we camped where she had marked a red flame, and shivered as we crawled under our blankets, lying close to our brushwood fire.

On the sixth morning, when I shaded my eyes and looked north, I could see what looked like water shimmering bright against the red land, about a quarter of a mile away. No, not water. Snow?

I had been thinking the salt lake was a salty lake. Such lakes do exist, here and there, saltier than the sea, salty as pickle brine.

The Arcaringa was a lake the way the Sleeping River was a river, an empty, dreaming place, waiting for the water.

And it was all salt. Crusted, white salt, cracked and broken the way you'd see a thin crust of silt cracked and broken at the bottom of a dried-up puddle. Acres and acres of salt. It would glare as brightly as the sky, once the sun was high.

Anna joined me, peering through her telescope. "No sailing on this lake," she said. I could tell she was surprised, too. "What do goblins look like?" she asked, after a moment.

"Goblins? They have gray skin and red eyes and are sort of hairy on their heads and shoulders, and their joints are knobby and crooked."

"Gray, not red?"

"Goblins are sandy red, like the desert," Kokako said. "*Sand*-goblins."

"Of course," I said wisely, as if I'd known that all along. I should have. It was obvious, really. "Goblins can't make themselves invisible the way most Old Things can. They just blend in with their usual landscape; they're camouflaged."

"These ones aren't," Anna said.

"Aren't what?" I asked.

"Camouflaged. They're red, and they're showing up very well against white salt."

"What goblins?" asked Kokako.

Anna pointed.

"Oh," he said, shading his eyes. We all stood looking at the goblins a moment, Anna studying them up close through the telescope, and Kokako and I watching them as not-that-distant reddish figures hurrying over the white salt.

Then we realized that if *we* could see *them* … we all flung ourselves flat on the ground. Jix screeched and tried to hide in Kokako's armpit.

Anna crouched back up on her knees, ready to leap upright. She drew her sword, and I took a firmer grip on my

spear. Kokako closed his hand on a rock. But the goblins hadn't seen us, after all. They don't like going out in sunlight, if they have any choice, and they actually see much better in dim light. As they drew closer, we could tell they were running towards something away to the east of us. We all scooted around to look.

"They're heading for that boulder," Anna whispered.

The boulder grew thinner and taller.

"That's the rock-man," hissed Kokako. "He must finally have come back to the sorcerer."

"They're pretty excited to see him."

"Probably Lord Barramundi's been getting mad about him taking so long," Kokako suggested. "It's too bad we didn't see him before the goblins did. I bet he could have told us about the *Oyon*."

"I thought he would only answer three questions," I said.

"He might have answered three more for you or Anna."

"Or he might have dragged us off to his master," Anna pointed out. "We can't trust the rock-creature, if he's being forced to work for Lord Barramundi." She watched through her telescope as the rock-man and the sand-goblins met and headed out into the salt again.

"They disappeared!" said Kokako.

"It looked to me like they jumped down into a hole," Anna said. "That must be the entrance to the goblin den."

"We should follow the goblins, shouldn't we?" Kokako asked. "The *Oyon*'s down there."

I felt an odd breeze tickling the back of my neck and rolled over, looking up into the endless blue—but the sky wasn't endless blue anymore. In the east, it looked hazy, dun-colored—a sort of brownish yellow, and gray above that. The mountains had curved back towards us as we headed north, so that we could see them again, blue and misty on the horizon, and the pale grass of the highlands. Now, though, all that was rapidly disappearing behind low, dark clouds.

Right beside me, the dust whirled up and dropped again. A clump of grass flattened itself. Another small whirlwind spun, tugging at my fur.

I could almost see something, a figure like the shimmer of heat in the air, tall and thin, almost spidery.

"Old Thing," a breath hissed in my ear. I sat up, and Anna turned to watch me, her head tilted to one side, frowning and squinting, as though she could almost see the creature, too. Another one joined it, and another, drawing up dust into hot, spinning columns. Wind Dancers.

"Danger," breathed one.

"A prisoner," hissed another. It was difficult for me to understand them. You know how language changes over time—you don't speak your language the same way people did three or four hundred years ago. Well, the Wind Dancers's accent was so ancient that even I had to listen closely, and think back a long, long way, to understand what they meant.

"Save her."

"Save who?" I asked.

"She cannot get out."

"We cannot get in."

"We will bring her out."

"Free her from the sorcerer."

"Free who?" I demanded.

"The Firebird."

"Firebird? What Firebird?" I asked. "We're here to find the *Oyon*." But the wind was rising, the sand whirling higher, sweeping around us, as the Wind Dancers grew more excited and anxious. They couldn't seem to help showing their emotions through their actions, like people who wave their hands around when they talk, and you know how people like that are always causing small disasters, knocking over teapots and sweeping breakables off shelves. The Wind Dancers had a whole desert to stir up.

Anna coughed and choked and pulled her scarf over her mouth and nose, and I hid my face in the fur of my arm. For what seemed like an hour, we lay there, trying not to breathe in too much dust, but it was probably only a few minutes. The wind's wailing died away and the stinging sand settled.

"What was that?" Anna asked, pulling her scarf away from her face. "Wind Dancers?"

"Yes," I said. "They want me—us—to rescue a Firebird. A *Firebird*. Even *I've* never met a real Firebird. They said something else, too. They said they couldn't get in and she couldn't get out, but that they'd bring her out."

"They're going to bring her out of the goblin den that they can't get into? How?" Anna asked skeptically.

"Oh," I said, looking back towards the east. "Look at that, Anna."

The distant clouds were growing, churning, turning the

black-blue color of a bruise. White flickers showed where lightning jumped between them, though we were too far away to hear the thunder.

"Rain in the highlands," Anna said slowly.

Rain was a pretty mild word for it. It looked like a savage storm to me. And between us and the highlands, the air was looking misty. The storm was coming this way.

"Wind Dancers can create thunderstorms by their dancing," I said. "At least, that's what a wombat told me. But I suppose they need a bit of moisture in the air to start with, and that's easier to find away from the desert. Magic always works best when it works with nature."

"Rain in the highlands," Anna repeated. "And it's not so far to the hills now. That kangaroo warned you against sleeping in the riverbed because of flash floods, and there's bound to be dry rivers here too, that would feed into the salt lake …"

I saw what she was thinking. "They're going to flood the goblin den and wash the Firebird out?" I was shocked. It seemed—extreme. Did they expect us to be able to save her from drowning, or—what a horrible thought, going out, like a campfire when water is poured on it? I didn't know anything at all about Firebirds. Maybe they could swim.

Anna suddenly looked around. "Where are Kokako and Jix?"

I looked around, too.

Kokako was gone. Again.

# CHAPTER TEN

# In which Kokako enters the sorcerer's lair

"We should follow the goblins, shouldn't we?" Kokako asked.

He jumped up and started to run, keeping his eyes fixed on the point where the goblins and the rock-man had disappeared, so that he wouldn't lose it in all the shining white salt. Jix flew on ahead, a bright, bobbing splotch of color. The parrot dropped down, and Kokako was close enough to make out a small heap of stones, all encrusted with salt so they were hardly visible. There was a dark, round hole in the ground, half covered with a flat slab of stone.

Jix squawked and flapped his wings. Probably that meant there were no goblin guards around. Probably they should have thought to look for guards before they went dashing off. Kokako peered down into the darkness. Probably a goblin doorstep was a bad place to sit being indecisive. He slid his legs over the edge of the hole, and dropped.

With a shriek, Jix plummeted after him, digging his claws into Kokako's shoulder just as Kokako landed on a smooth floor that wasn't as far away as he had suspected. He pitched forward onto his hands and knees, then picked himself up and got his back to the wall.

There were no goblins anywhere in sight. He was in a tunnel. The smooth, rounded walls, striped red and paler orange, had a strange glassy sheen, almost like pottery. Kokako remembered the rock-man saying his first task had been to make a house. He must have melted out this tunnel, following some flaw in the sandstone. The walls were rippled, bulging and curving.

Away from the opening in the roof, it was very dark. There was only one way to go, so Kokako started down the tunnel, which went on twisting and turning, opening off into small, rounded rooms and dead ends. In places, torches were fixed to the walls, giving a red, smoky light. The glassy ceiling was stained black with soot, and many of the rooms had crooked doors, roughly made out of bits of brushwood. It was easy to peer through the gaping cracks in them. In some of the rooms goblins were curled up, sleeping on beds that were nothing but heaps of dry grass and leaves. Kokako hadn't realized that they usually slept during the day. The ones he had followed must have been sent out to look for the rock-man.

Not all of them were sleeping, anyway. At a fork in the tunnel he could hear raised voices. It sounded like an argument. He flattened himself against the wall and peered cautiously around the corner.

The first thing he saw was the rock-man, sitting like a lumpy boulder with two glowing eyes beside an open door, if you could call that jumble of woven sticks a door. The rock-man's eyes dimmed and flared, and an arm grew out of his upper body, to point at Kokako. Or beyond? The other fork? Kokako started to back away, but froze where he was when he heard a human voice, raised in a roar.

"Because I said NO, that's why!"

"But we want to come, too!" That was a goblin's voice, raspy and whining. "Want to see the city. You promised, Lord Barramundi. Promised we could *have* the city for our own."

"I promised you could have a human town for your own.

Not a city, especially not Keastipol, and NOT YET."

"But we want to come this time. You let Dingobreath an' Seventoes an' Stonefang go to the city last time. It's not fair."

"I don't care if it's fair or not. First, letting Dingobreath and the others go was a mistake—they got lost and never came back, didn't they? Second, I'm traveling by sorcery and it's a bother trying to include goblins in the spell. And third—listen closely—the other cities' armies are marching towards Keastipol. Do you understand? Tomorrow I'm going to appear at the *Oyon*-Shrine like a hero. Their savior. The Peace-Bringer. All that Tero Korax the Wanderer ever gave them was an empty symbol, the *Oyon*—*I'll* bring the Firebird to them. I'll unite all the cities under one rule, stop all the arguing over nothing, and give them a *real* peace. But I can't stop their war and be acclaimed emperor if I show up with a bunch of scruffy, half-witted goblins tagging after me."

"Not half-witted," the goblin muttered.

"No? But that's what humans will say."

"Humans is stupid."

"Yes," Lord Barramundi said, and he sounded like he meant it, which puzzled Kokako, because it almost sounded as though the sorcerer didn't count himself as human. "They are. They're stupid and dangerous and anyone who isn't just like them is never good enough for them. But I'm going to become Emperor of the Great Southern Continent anyway." His voice changed, became velvety and kind. Kokako could almost believe he meant what he was saying. Maybe he did mean it. "They're not going respect me if I have a pack of goblins running after me everywhere, but *I* know you're all my good and faithful servants. And I always keep my promises. I'll let you have a human town for your very own—after I'm emperor."

"Tired of waiting," muttered the goblin, but it sounded a bit happier.

"Well, wait a bit longer."

Kokako jerked his head back as a tall man appeared in the doorway. *Stop their war?* It had happened, then. Annapurna Khanum wouldn't have reached Keastipol yet, and it was already too late. With the *Oyon* lost, the cities had given up arguing with one another in the Parliament of Seventy and gone to war instead.

Lord Barramundi strode around the corner. He stopped short when he saw Kokako, and then shot out his hand and grabbed him. Jix croaked and arrowed away.

"Hi," Kokako said brightly, smiling at the sorcerer's frown. "I'm lost."

Lord Barramundi looked at him as though he were some not-very-interesting beetle he'd found crawling on the floor. "You. I remember you. You were in the *Oyon*-Shrine. I thought Stonefang and his friends were going to eat you. Where are they?"

"I haven't seen them," Kokako said truthfully. "And you shouldn't go around telling goblins to eat people."

Lord Barramundi shrugged, as though it didn't matter much one way or the other. "There are plenty of people," he said. "One more or less won't make any difference."

"It will to me!" Arguing wasn't going to do him any good.

He should try to be harmless and innocent. "Can you tell me the way to the mountains?" Kokako asked hopefully.

"Do I look stupid?"

Actually, to Kokako, the sorcerer looked, a bit like his niece, Annapurna Khanum, and therefore not stupid in the least. He was very tall, with a thin, brownish face and narrow, beaky nose, and gold rings in both ears. He was dressed in a red velvet robe of the sort that magistrates and professors wore on formal occasions. His black hair and his short beard were streaked with gray, but he didn't look any older than Anna's mother, except for his eyes. They were a brilliant green, but they looked, to Kokako, old. Old and tired and angry, as though he had spent so long being angry that almost every other emotion had burned away or been forgotten. And one thing that looked very different were his teeth. Lord Barramundi's eye-teeth were just a little too long and a little too pointy, and made Kokako think of a dingo's fangs. He could see why some people might think Barramundi wasn't quite a proper human, with teeth like that. Other kids would pick on you for the stupidest little things, and once they started, it was awfully hard to make them stop. But that didn't mean you should make yourself a tyrant over them when you grew up. Kokako decided this wasn't a good time to tell Barramundi that. He tried to smile pleasantly, to try asking another question, but the sorcerer seemed to think he was finding something funny.

Barramundi shook him. "So you think I do look stupid enough to believe you're lost? We'll see how you laugh when Dingobreath and Stonefang and Seventoes show up looking for their supper."

He started walking again, dragging Kokako with him, down the other fork in the tunnel.

Kokako dug in his heels. He twisted and squirmed and beat at the man with his fists, but that did no good at all. Barramundi simply ignored him. He yelled and screamed, just in case Anna and Torrie were anywhere close, but that didn't help, either.

Lord Barramundi took a big key out of his pocket and opened a door that was nothing like any of the others Kokako had seen, being solidly built of heavy, dark boards, reinforced with iron straps. With a shove, he sent Kokako stumbling through and slammed the door. Kokako flung himself against it, but he didn't weigh enough to prevent the sorcerer closing it again. Nothing had ever sounded as final and hopeless as the *thunk* of the lock turning.

Kokako yelled, with his mouth to the keyhole, but nobody answered. He didn't expect them to, but he went on yelling. He had a heavy, sick feeling in his stomach, as he finally realized Anna and Torrie hadn't followed him after all.

Even Jix had deserted him. To be fair, he had to admit that was probably a good thing. Jix could bring the others to find him, if the parrot didn't get caught and eaten by a goblin first.

When his throat was raw and his voice hoarse, Kokako stopped yelling and sat with his back against the door. There were no torches lighting this room. The only light at all was sliding through the thin crack around the door, and it was so dim that it didn't do any good, except to show him where the door was. He couldn't even see the walls of the room.

He was supposed to be an explorer. Annapurna Khanum wouldn't sit down and give up. Anna wouldn't, either. If Anna or Torrie got locked up like his, they'd probably already be finding a way out. Kokako gathered his determination and got up, setting out to explore the room with one hand on the glassy wall. It curved. Pretty soon he came to the door again. He hadn't tripped over any furniture, but goblins didn't seem to go in for furniture much. He hadn't tripped over anything else, either. This, when he thought about it, seemed odd. The room had been locked before Lord Barramundi threw him in. There must be a reason: either something needed to be locked in, or the goblins needed to be locked out. The sorcerer might say he liked his goblins, but he had abandoned those three in the *Oyon*-Shrine pretty quickly, and nobody would trust goblins to stay honest and loyal around treasure. Every story he'd ever read said that.

And what treasure did Lord Barramundi have that needed to be locked up? On his hands and knees, Kokako began to feel his way over the floor, expecting to find something, a chest, a table, something that could hold the *Oyon*. What his hand touched, around the middle of the room, was smooth, slick cloth, a fabric that felt cold, almost oily, and seemed to stir and move by itself against his fingertips.

It was the dark cloth that the rock-man had thrown over the fire in the *Oyon*-Shrine, the blanket of utter night. The cold stung his fingers a little. Kokako took a firmer grip anyway and pulled at the blanket, but it didn't slide easily towards him. It wasn't merely covering a heavy lump, he realized; it was still gathered together at the top and tied, making a sort of sack. That made him suddenly furious. Lord Barramundi had stolen the *Oyon* and he didn't even bother to look at it? What did he want it for, then?

Kokako grabbed the bundle and tried to undo the cord tying it up. The cord made his fingers tingle and when he pulled at the knot with his fingernails, blue sparks danced and fizzed over his hands. He yelped and sucked his fingers. Then he tried again, but the knot and the cord stayed as firmly tied around the blanket as though the whole thing were one solid piece of carved stone.

The blanket didn't feel right, he realized, not if it were bundled around the *Oyon*. It was the wrong shape. He felt it carefully, and instead of the smooth oval of the *Oyon*, he felt something almost the same size, or maybe a bit bigger, but not such a regular shape. It was narrower towards one end, and had grooves and ridges. It felt as if it might be a carved stone, some sort of fantastical knotted-up creature, like the ones the people in his father's homeland of Whenualand carved on wooden posts to decorate their houses.

"What is this?" he asked aloud, and then he yelled again. "Where's the *Oyon*, you—you stupid sorcerer?"

"Kokako?" asked a voice. "Is that Kokako? Are you really out there? Can you hear me?"

# CHAPTER ELEVEN

# In which we get very wet

The storm came galloping out of the hills, rolling down on us like a herd of wild horses, but moving far more quickly than any horse ever did—faster than a bird could fly, fast as a hurricane wind. It drummed against the dry earth, and spray rose up from its leading edge like the foam on the curling lip of a wave, except this spray was red mud mixed with leaping, bounding white hailstones. Imagine a solid gray wall advancing across the landscape. *That's* what it was. And it would feel almost as solid when it hit us, too.

Already rain and melting hailstones were turning the ground dark, and pools were forming, finding channels that had been only dry depressions in the land. I could picture the water in the highlands, trickling down stony hillside ditches, curling around rocks, pools spreading, connecting, turning into a brook, a river moving almost as fast as the storm that fed it, towards its ancient end in the salt lake.

"Run!" I said. "We've got to get Kokako."

Anna didn't have to ask where he had gone. We both took off as fast as we could go for that tumbled heap of stones into which the rock-man and the goblin patrol had disappeared.

By the time we reached it, the white salt was already dissolving into slick, slippery mud, and our feet were already splashing in puddles up to our ankles. Anna slipped and went skidding along, just like a person falling on ice, and by the time I'd helped her up, we were both mud-coated and looked more like cousins to the rock-folk than anything.

I was not very happy to see that there was already a thin trickle of water finding its way down the hole.

A sand-goblin poked his head out, right as I was about to jump down.

"Hey!" he said. "What's going on? Where's all the water coming from?"

"The sky," I said.

Mouth open, the goblin stared up at the dark clouds in astonishment.

"But it rained just last winter," he said. "Hey, Stonefang ..." He beckoned me closer, and I realized he'd mistaken me for another goblin. I was going to set him straight in no uncertain terms, but Anna gave me one of those captain's looks, so I crouched down and let the goblin whisper, hissing and spluttering, in my ear.

"Is that Seventoes? He's gotten awfully tall. And what happened to Dingobreath?"

"Seventoes ate him," I said.

"Ate Dingobreath?" the goblin shrieked, staring in horror at Anna. "Ate her?"

"Ate her," I corrected, but he didn't seem to have noticed my mistake. "That's why Seventoes is so tall now. He grew."

The goblin wailed and dropped back out of sight.

"Come on, Seventoes," I said. "Let's go."

"Watch it, Stonefang," Anna said, drawing her sword. "Anyway, at least it's not Dingobreath. Let me go first."

"Alright."

Anna slid down into the hole, and I followed. I splashed into a puddle, which washed some of the worst lumps of red clay off, but didn't get me very clean, since the water was red with mud, too. We set off down a torchlit tunnel, following muddy goblin footprints. We could hear him in the distance, shouting.

"Lord Barramundi! Lord Barramundi! Stonefang and Seventoes are back at last, and Seventoes ate Dingobreath and he's five or six feet tall now, maybe eleven or fifteen, he's a giant! And *it's raining*."

"Raining?" we heard a human voice roar. "No!"

"Hide," said Anna, and we shoved open the nearest door, which was more a sort of woven screen of sticks, ducking into the little round room beyond, where a wrinkled old goblin was stirring something in a cauldron on a fire. There was no hole for the smoke to get out by, so the room was very thick and hazy and smelled like fish. I don't know where they got the fish.

"Hey!" the old goblin shouted, and she certainly didn't

mistake us for goblins. She hurled her iron ladle at me and I ducked, but it bounced off the wall and hit me. I yelped. It was hot, and fishy, and worst of all, iron, which for us Old Things is like poison ivy. That's the thing I hate about goblins, not their manners or their smell or the fact they eat anything and everything—iron and steel don't hurt them. It isn't fair. Makes me wonder if they're really Old Things at all.

Anna picked up the ladle and stood there with it in her left hand and her sword in her right.

"Quiet!" she ordered. "Don't move. Don't squeak. And you won't get hurt."

The goblin cowered down by her fire, and while Anna guarded her, I peered out through the cracks in the door, in time to see Lord Barramundi run by with the hem of his red robe hoisted up to his knees and a crowd of goblins scurrying after him.

Oh, oh, oh. I'd almost suspected it, when Annapurna had talked about her uncle having sand-goblin followers. Most sorcerers have more sense, but this one—I guess he liked the fact that it was easy to get goblins to look up to him and think he was wonderful. I recognized him, all right. We had met, oh, two or three times, in the past. And every time, he was up to some mischief, causing trouble somewhere.

And that solved one little mystery, one that had been bothering me ever since I first met Anna. Even though she wasn't a sorcerer, she had been able to see me when I hadn't meant her to. But if Lord Barramundi was her great-uncle—well, even a little drop of magic in the blood can do unexpected things.

"What is it?" Anna asked, seeing my face.

"Nothing," I said. "It doesn't matter right now. We need to find Kokako and get out of here before this place floods."

Anna gave the goblin a stern look and joined me at the door. "Is it all clear, can we go?"

"I think so," I said.

A shallow, glittering darkness of water was feeling its way down the tunnel, rushing ahead, pausing, finding a low spot and rushing again. It was only an inch or so deep, but it reminded me of the tide coming in across mudflats, and you know how dangerous that can be.

"Give me back my ladle!" the old sand-goblin howled as we left. "My stew's going to burn if I don't stir it!"

Anna threw the ladle back over her shoulder as we left.

More sand-goblins rushed past us, pushing and shoving on their way to the entrance.

"Cold!" they shrieked, when they splashed into the water. "Wet! Ugh!"

"Rock-man!" we heard the sorcerer bellow. "Get up here and make me a dyke, a wall to keep the water out. I command you, by your secret name! And bring me the Firebird!"

"Kokako!" Anna shouted. There didn't seem any point in trying to be sneaky. The sand-goblins were panicking. Some of them were carrying bundles over their shoulders. Lord Barramundi might think he could save his fortress, but the goblins didn't believe it. They knew the desert, and they knew what happened when it rained. For a sorcerer, he was sometimes very stupid. If he'd thought ahead at all, he'd have known this wasn't a good spot to dig a hole. I looked back once and saw our old goblin being carried along by some younger ones, still waving her ladle and shouting, "My cauldron, my good copper cauldron! Someone get my cauldron!"

"Look out!"

I pushed Anna up against the wall and flattened myself beside her. We felt a blast of heat, and the mud on our fur—my fur, I mean, and Anna's clothes—dried and baked solid, as the rock-man flowed up the tunnel towards us. It was like watching a broken-off chunk of hot lava crawling over the ground, with every crack and bend showing molten orange through the black. For a moment he turned glowing red eyes our way. One flickered. It might have been a wink. And then he was past and the deepening stream of water was steaming in his wake. It sizzled against him, filling the tunnel with mist, so that a cloud followed him as he vanished around a corner.

"Kokako!" Anna called again. "Check all the rooms, Torrie. If he's been captured, he might be tied up somewhere."

She took one side and I took the other, tearing open the badly made doors and peering in. She gave a yip of surprise at one, but it was only because Jix came hurtling out like he'd been shot from a catapult and crashed into her, grabbing hold of her shirt with his claws and trying to hide his head under her chin.

"Shh, shh, it's all right," Anna said, petting him. The poor bird was trembling.

"Goblins!" he said. "Goblins everywhere. They wanted to eat me!"

"That's what goblins are like," I said. "They always want to eat everybody. Come on, Jix. You're a mighty goblin fighter, right? Don't let them scare you."

"I'm not scared! I didn't say I was scared!"

"Of course not."

"There's so many of them! They caught me! But I fought them and I got away."

He was missing some of his nice blue tail-feathers, and he looked very ruffled.

"I'm sure you did. Stop trying to crawl under Anna's clothes and come show me where Kokako is."

Anna was trying to detach the parrot from her shirt front. She got him sitting on her wrist like a falcon and scratched his head. "It looks like he's been in a fight. I bet there are some goblins with sore noses."

Jix began to preen, straightening his feathers. If he had been a cat he would have purred.

"Kokako," I said firmly. "Where is he?"

Jix stopped looking so pleased with himself. "I don't know!" he wailed. "I lost him. That sorcerer caught him. I should have stayed. I should have fought him. I'm no good, I shouldn't have left him."

"Lord Barramundi captured him," I told Anna, and to Jix I said, "Stop that. Remember how brave you're supposed to be. Escaping the sorcerer was the right thing to do. It would have been better if you'd followed him so you knew where Kokako was, but it still means we have to rescue only one of you. Now show us where Kokako was captured."

Jix flitted ahead of us down the tunnel, now empty of goblins. The water had gotten ahead of us, and our feet splashed. It was up to my ankles now.

Actually, we had to rescue two. I wasn't forgetting about the mysterious Firebird. There was no way I was leaving her trapped down here when it flooded, and I thought the Wind Dancers' idea about washing her out with the water was a very bad one. Besides, I'd always dreamed of seeing—

"Right here," said Jix, at the fork in the tunnel you've already heard about. "This is where he was captured."

"Which way did the sorcerer go?" Anna asked, guessing what Jix's squawking and flapping meant.

Jix took the left-hand fork, and we followed. When we saw the heavy, well-made door, we knew we'd found the right place. It was locked, of course.

"I suppose you haven't learned to pick locks yet?" I asked Anna.

"Still haven't gotten around to it. How about you?"

I shook my head sadly.

"Stand back," said Anna, setting the point of her sword against the wood around the lock.

"You know," I pointed out, "you need to start carrying an axe."

≈≈≈≈≈

"Who's there?" Kokako demanded of the mysterious voice in the darkness. "Where are you? How do you know my name?"

"But I have known you for years. I remember your voice, and I learnt your name from the other voices who spoke to you. You read to me."

"Read to you?" Kokako asked in amazement. The voice certainly didn't belong to Jix, who was the only creature he'd ever read to since his grandmother died. It wasn't any sort of parrot squawking and croaking. It wasn't any sort of human voice, either. It was more like … music. Like singing, with a voice that flowed like a rich wooden flute.

"You sat by my egg and read to me, stories of traveling

and journeys and new lands." The voice sighed. "In my sleep I heard, and dreamed, and remembered. I remember such lands, from long ago."

"Your—egg?" Kokako squawked, sounding a lot like Jix. Compared to this voice, any human voice sounded a lot like Jix. "Who are you? Where are you?"

"I am ... the Firebird. And I think you are holding me in your hands. You must be, or I would not be able to speak to you through this blanket of utter night. I am trapped. I have waited so long to hatch again, and when finally the fire freed me from my sleep and I rose seeking the sky, I was trapped. The cold of utter night smothered me, froze my heart. It freezes me still, and I can do nothing but sit, and think, and remember. It is worse than the egg. The egg is a time for dreaming and remembering and rest, but now I am hatched: I need to fly, and see, and sing."

Kokako felt the cold, stinging sack carefully. It still seemed to hold a lumpish carving.

"You mean you're ... you're the *Oyon?*" he asked, not wanting to believe it. He remembered the old, formal name for it. If the Firebird were as old as she claimed, that might be the name she knew. "The *Oyon-Opallion?*"

"*Oyon-Opallion?* That means the opal egg, in the language of the first humans to come to the Great Southern Continent," the voice fluted thoughtfully. "I have never seen my own egg, of course. But perhaps it is made of opal."

"But it can't—you can't—*how?*" Kokako asked. "I don't understand anything. How can you have been in it if you laid it?

And anyway, it was given to us by Tero Korax the Wanderer. To bring peace. Nobody ever said it was alive."

"It is my egg because it is me," the voice said, sounding amused. "You sleep, and then you wake up, and you are still you, are you not?"

"I suppose …" It was hard to be upset, with that voice in his ears. It made him feel … calm. Deep. As though if he only thought a bit more carefully, he would understand so much more than he did now.

"The egg is like sleep, for me. I live for years and years, but I do not die. Instead, I make a nest of scented wood, and I burn."

"You burn yourself?" That horrified Kokako, no matter how hard he tried to understand.

"Ah, it is not like burning would be for you. You are a human, are you not?"

"Yes."

"For me, it is like …" The Firebird seemed to be thinking very hard, trying to remember things she had known long ago. "Like sinking into a warm bath at the end of a long, weary day. In the fire I am consumed, and I become an egg again. I rest, and I dream. And in time, there will be another fire."

"How?"

The Firebird laughed. "Lightning, foolish goblins, curious sorcerers, curious humans who want to see me and hear me sing. There will *always* be a fire, in time. And then I hatch and am reborn. But this time, I was trapped. I was not in the wilderness, where my friends the Wind Dancers might find me and bring me lightning. I was away from careless goblin fires, and it seemed no sorcerers or other humans remembered what I was, and so no one lit a fire for me."

"Lord Barramundi did."

"Yes. And then he had the poor enslaved rock-man, who would not be hurt by my burning touch, freeze me in the coldness of the night between the stars, which even I cannot warm."

Kokako tugged at the cord binding the blanket, or sack, or whatever it was, until his fingernails broke. Nothing did any good.

"I can't get the knot untied," he said. He might have sunk into despair then, except that the music of the Firebird's voice still lingered in his mind. It made him feel strong, and calm, and hopeful. "But I'll think of something."

The Firebird trilled a fragment of song without words, which seemed to warm his heart like a golden fire. His situation didn't seem so hopeless. If Torrie and Anna didn't show up before Lord Barramundi came back, he'd tackle the sorcerer around the ankles, grab the key from his pocket, take the blanket of utter night with the Firebird, and run. If he was fast enough, he could lock the sorcerer in and escape to find the others. Somehow, they could all figure out a way to free the Firebird.

"Why was your egg our *Oyon,* though?" he asked, after a while. "Didn't the Wanderer know what it was? It seems awfully cruel, to keep you as an egg forever."

"Tero Korax certainly never intended for me to be locked

in a temple and treated like a dead treasure," the Firebird said.

"So what happened?" Kokako asked. He started picking at the knot again, ignoring how it stung and burned his fingers.

"She came to me when I lay as an egg in the ashes of my nest far in the southwestern wilderness, and asked if I would sing for the people of the warring cities of the coast, to teach them to desire peace. I agreed. Even though I was within my egg, I could speak to her in dreams. She was one of the ancient ones, I think."

"Ancient ones? You mean Old Things, like my friend Torrie? But I've seen pictures of Tero Korax the Wanderer. Carvings. She was a human."

"Some Old Things look human. I think this sorcerer who has carried me off is not entirely human. It makes him angry, I think; he wishes humans to accept him as human, and at the same time he wishes to prove he is better than them. A very sad man."

"I did wonder about that," Kokako said. "He has weird teeth." But he decided he still didn't feel sorry for Barramundi in the least. "Well, if he's not entirely human, neither is his niece Annapurna. And she's not sitting around sulking about it. But Firebird, I don't understand. Back then, if Tero Korax wanted you to sing for the people, why didn't she light a fire for you, so you could hatch?"

The Firebird was silent for a moment, as though she was turning things over in her own mind. "I think," she said at last, "that Tero Korax left. I think she does not like to stay in one place for long. She is the Wanderer. I think a magistrate of

Keastipol was to make my fire, once the magistrates and the chief men and women from the other cities arrived. But," and her voice fluted wordlessly again, sounding thoughtful, and a little sad, "I think that the one magistrate, who understood what my egg was and what I was and what the Wanderer hoped my song could show them, was a very old man. And he died, as very old men sometimes do."

"So nobody knew?"

"It seems to me that is what must have happened. I know Tero Korax the Wanderer did not intend for me to be imprisoned and turned into an icon, worshipped with no understanding."

"She should have written a note," Kokako said. "But," he added, "you did bring peace. There hasn't been a war in a hundred years, although we've come awfully close, sometimes."

"How?" the Firebird asked. "How, when I was only a pretty stone?"

"People *believed* they could have peace. You—your egg—was a reason to believe it could happen," Kokako guessed. That seemed to him to make a kind of sense. "So they worked harder at it. But now, there's going to be war again. Because people think I destroyed the *Oyon*, and the other cities are blaming Keastipol. Lord Barramundi must have stolen—kidnapped—you, to start a war."

"He wants to stop a war," the Firebird corrected. "He told me so."

"But all he's done is start one."

"And then he can stop it."

"Oh." Kokako considered that. "I see. I guess I heard him saying something like that. He wants to be like the Wanderer all over again, only better." And what else had the sorcerer said? "He wants to make himself emperor," Kokako said indignantly. "We don't have kings or emperors here."

"Then you had best free me, so he cannot carry me to Keastipol and claim me as his great gift to the people," the Firebird said.

"Torrie will have an idea how to get this knot untied," he said. "He knows about magic. We'll escape and find him as soon as someone opens the door."

A moment later he added, "I think I'm sitting in a puddle. It's getting deeper. And what's the gnawing noise?"

# Chapter Twelve

# In which we get even wetter

The gnawing noise was us. Chips and splinters flew as Anna dug at the wood around the lock with her sword. Jix hopped from foot to foot with nervousness. Water swirled around our legs, and rose higher and higher. If the rock-man had built a wall or dyke around the entrance to the tunnel, either he had done a very poor job, or the lake was flooding faster than he or Lord Barramundi expected. I suppose the sorcerer had no idea just what angry Wind Dancers were capable of. I know I didn't. I was starting to be a bit worried.

"Let me try," I said, and I dug the tip of my spear into the wood and started chipping away at it too.

"Kokako!" I called. "Are you in there?"

"Torrie?" his voice answered. "Anna? Is that you?"

Jix jumped up and down, shrieking and flapping his wings.

"And Jix," I said. "We're trying to cut the lock out."

"Hurry," Kokako called. "We have to set the Firebird free before Lord Barramundi can take her to Keastipol and make her sing for him."

"What did he say?" Anna asked, grunting with the effort as she levered a huge splinter free. Her sword was growing dull. Swords aren't meant for chopping wood, a fact Anna needed to write on the back of her hand so she'd remember, since she seemed to end up doing it so often. "A Firebird again? I thought they were legends." She paused to wipe her forehead and grin at me.

"Speaking as a legend myself, I've never seen one either," I admitted.

The water was up to my waist now.

"Kokako, how deep is it in there?" I called.

"Up to my ankles. Is it raining?"

"That's one way of describing it," said Anna.

I suppose the door fit so tightly that it was keeping the water from flowing in too quickly. But it would still fill the room before long, and if we hadn't gotten the door open by then, Kokako would drown. So would we, probably.

Ribbons of mist coiled past me. I turned to look, and saw a bank of fog approaching—fog, or steam. Two pits of red light loomed out of the fog like lanterns on a ship.

"Move," the rock-man rumbled. Anna and I both moved in a hurry. The water around him *boiled*.

"Away from the door, little human," he boomed, and then he leaned on the door.

Have you ever held a straw in the flame of a candle? The

door caught fire and burned through, just like that. *Fwoomph.* Ashes and sizzling bits of melted iron were swept into the room as the deep water from the corridor poured through in churning rapids. We heard Kokako shout in a sort of watery, gurgling way, and plunged into the room ourselves. Anna pulled him up out of the water, but Kokako gasped, "Let go!" and dove under again. He seemed to be looking for something. When he reappeared, he was clutching a bundle that seethed and shimmered with magic, to my eyes. It was covered with crawling purple shadows, a cold and dangerous magic, not something I'd ever want to touch, and it spat sparks that even the humans could see every time Kokako's fingers came near the cord binding it closed.

"Is that the *Oyon*?" Anna asked, taking Kokako's free hand as he slung the bundle over his shoulder. She sheathed her sword and gave me her other hand. It was safer to cling together, in case one of us slipped. The water tugged and pulled at us.

"The Firebird," Kokako panted. "She was the *Oyon*. It was an egg, and nobody remembered." And he told us most of the rest of it as we struggled through the rising water, following the rock-man back towards the entrance. We couldn't follow too closely, and the water was still hot as tea as it swirled and churned around us.

"Hurry," the rock-man called back, more than once.

One by one, the torches went out, splashed or even swamped by waves. I had to climb up piggyback on Anna, and Kokako's head disappeared beneath sudden surges as the current changed and fought itself. Jix just shut his eyes and held on, repeating, "Tell me when it's over," again and again. Odds and ends abandoned by the sand-goblins floated around us: sticks from broken doors, charred branches from fires, ragged bits of soggy clothing, a basket of dead frogs—maybe that stew had been frogs instead of fish.

It became obvious there was no other way out of the tunnel. The water, rather than flowing through, was hitting the farthest end and storming back. It was too easy to imagine the level rising higher, to imagine it filling all the space above us so that there was no air, no way out, water rushing into our mouths, filling our lungs …

"Light," gasped Anna thankfully, and we floundered to it, clambering only with great difficulty up the waterfall the entrance hole had become. At least the water was cleaner now, and washed off a lot of the mud that still covered Anna and me.

The rock-man's wall was amazing. It was a low ridge circling the heap of stones that marked the entrance, and it was made of rock he must have called up out of the earth. Lava, in fact. It was black and rough and steaming. The water poured over it at one low place, just enough to flood the tunnel and keep Lord Barramundi from being able to use it anymore, but not enough to flood it quickly, I realized. It had seemed pretty rapid to us, since we were inside when it happened. But it could have been much worse.

We climbed over the hot stone dyke and waded, half-swimming, to the nearby shore. Goblins bobbed and splashed, swimming in the lake. Far to the west, a ragged band of more goblins straggled along the water's edge, carrying bags and bundles.

They'd probably never get that copper cauldron back, though.

Already the storm clouds were breaking up. The sun was shining through, making the shallow lake dance and glitter, and the red land gave off coils of mist. Within a few days, it would be bright with sudden new growth, flowers carpeting the ground, trees blooming, frogs waking to lay eggs in the shallow lakes and ponds, birds singing and nesting quickly while the green days lasted. And then it would all dry and fade and sleep again. The land would be brown and yellow and red, and the lake would seep into the earth and evaporate into the air, leaving its salt behind in a new white crust.

Lord Barramundi wasn't thinking about the transformation of the land. "I told you to bring me the Firebird!" he roared at the rock-man. "Where is she? And your dyke wasn't high enough!"

"Didn't say how high," the rock-man rumbled.

"Where's the Firebird?"

The rock-man seemed to tower up, growing taller, even heavier, as though he were pulling more magma from beneath the earth. "Bound to three tasks," he said. "No more. I take back my name now."

And to my eyes, something did seem to flicker between the sorcerer and the rock-man, a sort of swirl in the air. Lord Barramundi snatched at it, but his hand didn't even come close. The rock-man turned our way. He gave a little bow, a sort of solemn nod of his head, and then he shrank down and stretched, becoming longer than he was tall. In that shape, he went speeding off towards the west and the deeper desert.

"I wonder what's out there?" Kokako, distracted, sounded a bit wistful as he watched the rock-man fade into the distance.

"One adventure at a time," said Anna.

That was when Lord Barramundi spotted us, or spotted the blanket of utter night Kokako carried.

"Brat!" he bellowed. "That's mine!"

He started striding along the shore towards us, but his long wet robes clung and tangled around his legs, and he stumbled. We didn't have time to laugh while he picked himself up.

"Help me!" Kokako said. "I can't get the knot undone and we have to set her free."

Anna pulled out her knife, but the moment she touched it to the knot it sparked and flared so that she dropped it.

"Quick, oh, quick," Kokako implored.

"Let me." I didn't like the look of the cord that bound the blanket at all. It seemed to me a nasty, ugly sort of magic, worse than the blanket itself. But my spear was made for fighting dragons, and it has its own magic, deep in the bronze. I slid the point under the cord and twisted, and the rope, or whatever it was, parted like rotten yarn. The blanket fell down, opening out like a flower.

For a moment, we were looking at a softly glowing stone. It was milky white, shot through with shimmering streaks of orange and green and red. It seemed to be the odd, pointy, lobed shape of a heart, but far too large. Then it looked like an intricately carved falcon all coiled up on itself, and then it was both at once, all in the space of one breath.

Then it burst into a roaring pillar of flame and the Firebird

rose into the sky like a fountain.

She was beautiful. I had heard stories, but I had never imagined she could be so awe-inspiring. She was about the size and shape of an eagle, but long plumes trailed back from her head and tail and the edges of her wings, and she was not flesh and blood and bone and feathers, but fire and light, gold, copper, bronze, scarlet, with streaks and sparks of green and purple.

"Thank you, Kokako," she called as she disappeared, becoming nothing more than a trail of light, like a comet, lost in the glare of the sun. Swirls of mist and shimmering air rose after her: the Wind Dancers, following to dance with her in the sky.

We stared where she had been, forgetting all about the danger, forgetting the sorcerer. Lord Barramundi was staring, too, his face twisted ugly with rage. But he didn't forget we were there.

"You!" he bellowed, turning on us. "You again!" In a few more quick strides he stood almost in front of us. And he raised his hands, muttering in one of those secret languages sorcerers make, to keep other people from learning their spells.

It might have been me he meant by "You again"; it might have been Kokako. I couldn't tell, and there wasn't time to worry about it. I jumped in front of both the humans and raised my spear to throw.

"Uncle!" Anna shouted.

That surprised the sorcerer. For a moment he looked like a fish, mouth gaping, eyes goggling.

"Great-Uncle," Anna corrected herself politely. She put a

hand on my shoulder and stepped around me, pushing me a little sideways. My foot hit the bitter cold of the blanket of utter night and I flinched away. Anna kept walking forward. Behind her back, her hand waggled at Kokako and me, pointing. Then she held it out, offering to shake hands. "We haven't met before. I'm Anna, captain of the cog *Shrike*. I'm your niece Annapurna's daughter."

She actually managed to take Lord Barramundi's hand, he was so astonished. "It's so wonderful to meet you at last," she said, edging sideways, so that the sorcerer had to turn a little away from us to face her. "I've heard so much about you from, oh, Mother, Grandmother, all the relatives …"

"What relatives?" he snarled, snatching his hand away. "I don't have any relatives except my interfering sister, and if you're her granddaughter, I doubt you've heard anything at all about *me*." Barramundi pushed up his sleeves. "And I don't care if we are related, if you're in league with that annoying brat from the *Oyon*-Shrine and that—that—that friend of my sister's, that smug, sneaking, hairy *Torrie*, I'll deal with you as you deserve."

"Friend of his sister's?" Kokako repeated in surprise, looking at me.

I was, sort of—although that's neither here nor there, at the moment, but another story entirely.

"You know Anna's grandma?"

"Never mind," I whispered. "Move slowly, so he doesn't notice. This way." I took Kokako's wrist and tugged him a little farther out of Barramundi's field of vision. I think just then we could have been dancing hornpipes and singing sea shanties, and he wouldn't have noticed. Which, of course, was exactly what Anna intended.

Lord Barramundi began chanting a spell again, but this one sounded different from before. Bad as he could be, I didn't think he was really going to hurt his great-niece. At least, I was pretty sure he wouldn't kill her. Anna was gambling on that, too. Nevertheless, she flinched as thick, sticky threads began to spin themselves around her, as if invisible spiders were circling. She tried to move her hand to the hilt of her sword, but her arms were already bound tightly to her body.

Kokako started to cry out and spring towards her, but I grabbed him back. He looked at me as though I had committed a horrible betrayal, and I held my breath, but the sorcerer still didn't look our way.

"Wait," I told Kokako, speaking softly. I picked up the blanket of utter night, which was right at our feet. Frost crackled on it.

Now, Kokako understood. We each took an edge of the blanket. "On three," I whispered. "One, two—three!"

We hurled the blanket of utter night up and over Barramundi's head. He let out one wailing howl as it settled, flowing in a silky, oily way right down around his boots, clinging to him. I grabbed him around the ankles and tipped him over and Kokako quickly sat on him while I tied up the blanket below his kicking feet. I didn't use the horrible magical cord, but the leather thong I pulled off Anna's braid. It would do. I may not be a sailor, but when I tie a knot, it stays tied.

Barramundi stopped kicking and howling. He stopped moving at all. Kokako jumped up, his face gray. "Is he …?"

I felt the blanket, carefully. It was cold, cold, cold. Lord Barramundi felt like a marble statue, but even as I started to say, "I think he's frozen," the statue began to shrink and draw in on itself. The blanket shrank with it. All I could feel now was a cold, roundish stone, about the size of a man's fist. It was just barely possible to feel details in the shape of it, head and arms and legs all tucked close together, curled up like a sleeping baby. Like the Firebird, Lord Barramundi had been chilled down to an ember, or maybe you could call it his heart. But the Firebird was full of joy and fiery life, so the ember that had held all her life had been much bigger, even though she was so much smaller than Barramundi.

"His heart's still here," I said. "He isn't dead. I think."

"What now?" Kokako asked, sounding a bit nervous.

"Me!" said Anna, with a bit more of a squeak than her voice usually had. "Quickly."

I used my spear, and Kokako used his little knife, to cut the sticky, clinging cobwebs away from her.

"Ahhhh," Anna said. "Ugh." She scraped thick cobweb off her face, flicking her hands to free them from the last sticky strands. "Ohhhh, I'm never going to feel the same way about spiders again."

"Why didn't you use your sword?" Kokako asked. "You could have told him to stop chanting or you'd cut off his head!"

"I thought confusing him would be a better distraction," Anna said, rubbing at the horrible cords that still clung in bits and pieces to her arms. "Besides, I guess he is a relative. Although he certainly deserved to be turned into a lump of rock." She frowned, and tugged at her braid, which was already starting to come undone. "Now what do we do with him?"

I picked up the blanket—it was more like the pillowcase of utter night, now, but that doesn't sound so poetic—and jiggled it. It didn't weigh very much, only a couple of pounds. All that anger and bitterness and it all came down to this, a lump of rock. And it probably wouldn't be beautiful opal, although I wasn't about to peek inside to check. I sucked on my fingers, which already felt as if frost had nipped them. Then I tied the bag to my spear, like a tramp's bundle, so I could carry it over my shoulder without touching it.

"What do we do with him?" I repeated Anna's question, and shook my head. I had no idea.

Anna scratched her head, pulling off more cobweb. "I suppose he's harmless for now, at least. Let's go, before the goblins notice. They might want him back."

Most of those that had been in the water seemed to be struggling out on the opposite shore of the lake. A few of them hadn't made it, unable to swim, maybe, or drowned as the cave flooded. Stupid Barramundi. He'd probably simply thought the salt lake was an interesting, different sort of place to make his lair, never considered what might happen when it did rain again. I stood soberly watching for a moment as two goblins struggled to drag a heavy, still body out on the far shore. I could hear one of them wailing, faintly. I've killed goblins in battle, to save the lives of my friends. It doesn't mean I think their lives don't matter.

Anna and Kokako were already walking away, with Jix perched atop Kokako's head like a prickly-toed hat. Neither of them seemed to give a second thought to the dead goblins. They were human. Goblins weren't. Or maybe they just hadn't noticed. I turned and hurried after them.

"Why so gloomy, Kokako?" Anna was asking, as I caught up.

He scuffed his sandal in the mud. "No *Oyon* to take back to Keastipol," he said. "I'm glad the Firebird's free, but there's still no proof I didn't burn a hole in the roof of the *Oyon*-Shrine and destroy the *Oyon*. It's not as though having a lump of stone wrapped up in a cold blanket is going to make Chief Magistrate Jabiru believe me. And Lord Barramundi's war might be starting. We haven't managed to change anything."

"Well, at least the Firebird's free," Anna repeated. "Wherever she's gone to."

Just then, that seemed the only thing to be glad about.

≈≈≈≈≈

We were a mile from Arcaringa Salt Lake, heading for the mountains, when we saw three bedraggled figures coming towards us.

Sand-goblins.

"Sand-goblins!" shrieked Jix, and took to the air.

"Somehow, they don't seem so worrying anymore," Kokako said, picking up a stick.

"Stonefang, Seventoes, and Dingobreath?" Anna guessed.

They looked tired, dusty, and muddy, slouching along scuffling their feet. As we drew closer, we could hear them arguing.

"I told you, we should have gone left at the split rock, Stonefang."

"You said right, Dingobreath."

"I didn't!"

"You did. I said, 'We go left here, do we?' and you said, 'Right,' so I went right."

"I said, right, meaning right, *correct*, we should go left. Idiot."

"Idiot, yourself, why did you follow me, then?"

"Hey!" said the tallest goblin. "This isn't right!"

"It isn't left, either, Seventoes. We're going straight on, till we reach the salt lake. Numbskull."

"No, I mean, this is wrong. Look! It's a lake."

"Yes, listen carefully. Salt. Lake. Arcaringa Salt Lake."

"But it's water!" screeched Seventoes desperately, and both the others looked up.

"And humans! With a sword!"

"And an Old Thing!"

"With a spear!"

They started to run away.

"Hey!" I shouted, cupping my hands around my mouth. "The others went that way!" I pointed to the western end of the lake. One of them did look back, and all three veered away towards the west, so I felt a bit better.

Jix came back, swooping to land on Kokako's shoulder. "Did you see them run? They probably remembered me from the *Oyon*-Shrine."

"You've saved us all," I said.

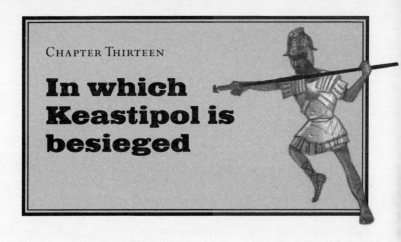

CHAPTER THIRTEEN

# In which Keastipol is besieged

W e had a few more adventures on our journey back to Keastipol, but nothing we couldn't handle. At least there weren't any crocodiles. Almost as worrying as crocodiles would have been, though, were the stories we heard from other human travelers on the road, about armies from the other cities marching to Keastipol, or sailing along the coast.

After we'd heard that story for the third time, and decided it must be true, we couldn't walk fast enough. Luckily, armies don't move very quickly, what with all their tents and armor and baggage and things.

Still, they moved too quickly for us.

On a clear afternoon with a hot wind blowing, we came over the last rise and looked down a long sweep of road towards the city wall of Keastipol, with its streets of gray limestone and white marble houses, all square and flat-roofed. On the high, steep hill at the edge of the city, the *Oyon*-Shrine dazzled our eyes. It still had a hole in its roof. Much closer to us were the glint of bronze and steel, the bright rainbow colors of banners and tents, silk and canvas snapping in the wind. The olive groves and the vineyards were crowded with tents, and with people— soldiers. And the city gates of Keastipol were shut.

"They didn't listen to Annapurna Khanum," Kokako said, as if he couldn't quite believe it.

"Or something happened to prevent her getting to Keastipol," Anna said grimly, but she didn't suggest that her mother might have forgotten all about her mission, and gone off on another exploration.

"Maybe you should send Jix to let the crew know we're back," I suggested. We obviously weren't going to be getting into the city any time soon.

"We have to talk to the magistrates ourselves," Kokako said. "Maybe if they see Torrie, they'll believe me." But he didn't sound as if he had much hope of it.

"Will there be magistrates with the armies from the other cities?" Anna asked.

"Bound to be," Kokako said. "Probably in the camps, there, telling everybody what to do."

"Right, then. We'll talk to them. And maybe Flytch can talk to the ones inside. Someone's got to make them see sense, and I suppose we can't expect Tero Korax the Wanderer to show up again."

Anna tore a page out of her notebook and scribbled a quick

message with the stub of a pencil. Kokako peered under her elbow. It seemed to cheer him up, or maybe it was just that Anna had a plan. Things always look better, when you have a plan.

"You think anyone's going to be able to read that?" he asked. "Maybe I should write the note."

"There's nothing wrong with my handwriting."

"*Fly war brrrl.W hrv t stp th— wrr. Cmm t tr gate nl tll tm ...?*" read Kokako.

"*Flytch, we're back. We have to stop this war. Tell the Chief Magistrate and the others I've got proof it was a sorcerer took the Oyon, and bring them to the gate. We'll talk to the ones outside. P.s. Have you seen my mother? She was supposed to talk to the magistrates and stop the war and wait for me on Shrike*," said Anna. "It's perfectly clear."

"Of course, Mister Flytch isn't as young as he used to be," I said, turning the scrap of paper upside down to see if it made any better sense that way. It didn't.

"Maybe he could borrow Annapurna Khanum's eyeglasses," Kokako suggested, grinning despite his worry.

"Shut up, both of you," said Anna. "Tell Jix to hold still." She rolled the note up tightly and pulled a thread from the hem of her shirt to tie it to the parrot's leg. We watched as he wheeled away, heading for the harbor.

It was obvious to me that the armies hadn't been there more than a day or so. It doesn't take an encamped army long to cut down all the nearby trees for their cooking fires, and trample all the green things to muck, but that hadn't happened yet.

"What are they doing down there?" Kokako asked, shading

his eyes against the glare of the sun and staring down at the city gates, with their round towers guarding them.

Anna pulled out her telescope for a better look. I shaded my eyes as Kokako had done. There was suddenly a strange, hollow, tired feeling in my stomach. We might not have time to talk to anyone.

Gleaming bronze helmets. Soldiers with shields and swords and long spears, marching slowly forward. Trumpets blaring a challenge, and drums beating time, as more soldiers, dozens of them, leaned forward, heaving on thick ropes. There were oxen there, too, yoked in pairs. And creaking as they bumped along behind the men and women and oxen were catapults and tall wooden siege towers, as high as the battlements of the city walls. Carts rumbled behind, pulled by more oxen, carrying rounded stones—shot for the catapults. The wheel of one of the towers caught in a ditch. For a moment it swayed, tottered. We all held our breath. And then slowly, like a tree when the woodsman strikes the last blow with his axe, it leaned, leaned … soldiers were already running away … crashed, smashing itself to bits. Oxen bellowed, still hitched to the wreckage, and someone ran back to free them.

But the other towers and the catapults kept moving. When they stopped, with the towers a little behind, the soldiers became very busy about them.

"What are they doing?" Kokako asked. "What's going on?"

"They're going to try to bash a gap in the wall," Anna said. "Then they can rush in through the hole. Or maybe, if they can weaken a corner of one of Keastipol's towers, it'll fall."

"And the wooden towers are so they can get over the city walls," I added. "Two different ways to get in."

"And then what?" Anna muttered. "Tear Keastipol apart looking for the *Oyon*, just in case it's hidden somewhere after all? Start killing people if they can't find it?"

"Probably," I said. "But there'll be people getting killed long before then, if we don't do something."

I wondered if Keastipol had any of those gilded mirrors on the towers of the city wall, like they did on the ones that overlooked the harbor, for burning enemy ships. From where I was, I didn't see any. The weapons they already had here would be quite enough. Lots of people on both sides were going to be horribly injured or even killed. I gave the heavy bundle of the blanket of utter night an angry shake. Stupid Barramundi. Right then, I really wanted to wait until *Shrike* was out in the middle of the ocean somewhere, and throw him overboard. But I knew I wouldn't. I'm not that kind of Thing. And not that it made what he'd done any less wrong, but it was true Barramundi hadn't meant to let the war actually happen, just as he hadn't meant to get some of his sand-goblin followers drowned. He simply didn't think enough and didn't care enough about what his greed for power over other people ended up doing to them.

And then, as we watched, not sure what we should do, the first catapult shot, its great arm jerking forward and suddenly stopping, flinging the stone—it arched up and fell short, kicking up a huge clump of mud. The catapult crew bustled around their machine, hauling the arm back, making adjustments. A second shot, and this one struck the city wall. We heard the *thunk* of it, and I thought I saw chips of stone fly. The attackers cheered. Then all the catapults were letting fly, aiming at the same point on the wall, to batter it to bits, and ones from Keastipol were answering them. A flight of arrows hissed down, hitting nothing but grass—the attackers were still too far away. A well-aimed bolt from a ballista atop a tower in Keastipol struck one of the catapults and shattered its arm. Defenders on the walls cheered.

"They *can't*," said Kokako desperately. "I can't let them do this." He took off running, not across the side of the hill to the camp, but down the dusty white road towards the battle.

"Hey!" shouted Anna, and she raced after him. I followed, but she had longer legs. Then the wind plucked and tugged at my fur. It hummed and sang in the roadside weeds and in my ears, and I realized it was trying to get my attention.

I squinted my eyes and looked out over the baking, dry grass between the olive trees. The air shimmered in an odd, twisty, spidery pattern.

"Er, hello?" I said.

"Old Thing of the north," whispered the wind, but of course it was a Wind Dancer. "I carry a message."

"For me?" I asked politely, with an anxious eye on Anna and Kokako. Anna had caught up with him, but he wouldn't stop. When she tried to grab his arm, he jerked it away angrily and ran on. Anna had no choice but to follow him. And I could see soldiers noticing them now, pointing … there were people on the walls pointing, too. "Could you be quick?" I asked. "I think there's about to be an emergency."

"Tell the smallest human that if he calls her, the Firebird will come to him. She says, if he needs her, he only has to ask and she will help, because he is her friend."

"I'll tell him," I said. "I don't suppose you'd like to blow up a good fog, or something, to stop this battle from happening? Or maybe a storm so everybody will hide in their tents?"

"No," said the Wind Dancer. "Human foolishness is not our concern." The grass whirled wildly around us, and then it was gone.

Too bad. A good thunderstorm might have settled everything. A few lightning strikes on the catapults ... but this wasn't my piece of the world, and it wasn't up to me to call down lightning.

I ran after Anna and Kokako and caught up, invisible to all other humans. The reason I caught up was that they seemed to have been arrested. Or not quite arrested. Anna was standing in front of Kokako with her sword drawn, but she was facing eight men and women in armor. Everyone looked extremely angry, and several of them held drawn bows.

"Spying on the camp!" their leader accused Anna.

"We weren't!" Kokako said indignantly. "We were—"

"I would hardly call running into the middle of a battlefield spying," said Anna coldly. "I'm Captain Anna of the ship *Shrike*, and my friends and I have proof that the *Oyon* wasn't destroyed by a seven-foot-tall hunchback, or stolen by another city, or hidden by Keastipol, or whatever they're saying now."

"Sure you do," said the leader rudely. "Where's your proof?

And where are your friends? I only see one kid."

Anna gave him a slow, nasty smile. "You'll have to wait and find out," she said, as though she had the olive groves packed full of cunningly disguised pirates, ready to spring out. "But you should know I'm on a mission for the Crown Prince of the Granite Isles. Do you want to upset the pirate-queen? Your magistrates aren't going to be very impressed with you, if you annoy her. Do you know how big a fleet of war-galleys the Granite Isles has? You'll probably find yourselves demoted to— to street-sweepers."

"Better take them to the magistrates," a woman suggested, looking a bit worried.

"An excellent idea," said Anna. "I want to see all the magistrates. That means What's His Name from Keastipol, too."

"And the city council," said Kokako. "We need to see Chief Magistrate Jabiru and the Keastipolian city council, too."

"I rather think the magistrates have more important things to do than meet with foreigners," the leader said.

"But we have to stop this," Kokako protested. "You don't really want a war, do you?"

"Maybe we can let them go," said another soldier. "Nobody said we had to arrest foreign sea captains."

"Nobody said we should let them go, either. What if it was foreigners who destroyed the *Oyon,* eh? Did you think of that?"

"That sounds like something someone from Keastipol would say."

"Don't be ridiculous. I grew up two houses over from you."

"Ah, but you might have become a Keastipolian spy."

"If I had, I certainly wouldn't give myself away by saying things only someone from Keastipol would say."

"Well, if only someone from Keastipol would say the *Oyon* was destroyed by foreigners, and you just said it, then logically, that means you must be from Keastipol."

"I'm your cousin, idiot!"

"Don't call me idiot! I outrank you!"

"Both of you shut up," the leader said to the two who were squabbling. And in that moment Kokako dodged the one nearest him and took off running again.

"Don't you dare!" Anna screamed at the woman who spun around, bow drawn, and with the flat of her blade she struck down on the soldier's left arm, so the bow jerked towards the ground and the arrow sank harmlessly into the road.

"I didn't mean—" The soldier dropped her bow, her face going gray when she realized that by reacting without thinking she'd almost shot a young boy.

None of the others in the patrol knew what to do. There were eight of them; they could have overcome Anna easily, but they were all so shocked by what had almost happened that they could only stand there while Anna glared at them, sword in hand. She gave me a nod and I ran after Kokako.

"We have proof it was a sorcerer who stole the *Oyon*," I heard her repeating behind me, in her most commanding captain's voice. "Send for the magistrates. Then whatever happens, it won't be your fault."

It was going to be my fault, though, if Kokako got mashed

by a shot from a catapult or skewered by a stray arrow, or even worse, killed on purpose by someone like that soldier, who simply saw someone running and thought *enemy* without thinking at all. I should have hung on to him.

∿∿∿∿∿

But maybe the people of the Great Southern Continent weren't as thoughtlessly warlike as they used to be, because nobody shot Kokako, and when they realized that there was someone, a mere boy, out in the open space before the city gates, first one and then another of the crews on the great engines of war stopped what they were doing.

"Don't be so stupid!" Kokako shouted, but his voice was just a thin, faint sound in all that great space. "It was a sorcerer who stole the *Oyon-Opallion*. And anyway, it wasn't supposed to be kept like a treasure, it was an egg, it was supposed to hatch ..."

"Wait till Anna brings the magistrates," I panted, catching up to him at last. I untied the small, heavy bundle of the blanket of utter night from my spear and set it carefully at my feet—just in case I needed the spear for other things.

"They've stopped," Kokako said, sounding a bit stunned. "I stopped them."

"And we're going to be in real trouble if they start again," I muttered under my breath. "Hurry up, Anna."

A trumpet bleated and blared—behind us. We both looked over our shoulders. A gate was opening. Not the big, iron-bound city gates, but what they call a sally port, a little, well-defended doorway a bit off to the side, that's meant for dashing out of and surprising the enemy. Nobody was dashing, though. Instead, a very nervous-looking trumpeter came out, with a very nervous-looking man beside her carrying a tall staff with green branches tied to it. Olive branches, which are a symbol of peace, or at least, a symbol of a truce and a parley, just like a white flag.

Behind them came …

"Chief Magistrate Jabiru!" hissed Kokako in surprise. "And some of the other city councillors. And some of the city watch."

And, in that crowd of mostly dark faces, a few sunburnt red and brown ones, too—Mister Flytch, Mirimick, and

Annapurna Khanum. Jix shot away from her shoulder and landed on Kokako's, nuzzling a beak into his hair.

"We've been told an emissary from the one who stole the *Oyon* wishes to speak to us," the Chief Magistrate said huffily. "Where is he?"

"Oh, that was a lie." Annapurna Khanum gave everyone a cheerful smile and patted the Chief Magistrate's pudgy arm. "But since you've been refusing to believe the truth no matter how often I tell it, I decided you'd probably be happier with a lie. And it got you out here, didn't it? Now, I think my daughter's friend here needs a chance to tell you all what actually happened to your *Oyon*. And I want to hear about it, too, so why don't we all sit down?" She winked at Kokako and plunked herself down on the grass, looking perfectly relaxed and at home.

Nobody else sat down. Chief Magistrate Jabiru looked as if he might explode. He spun around to head back to the sally port, but somehow there was a large pirate—Banksy the carpenter—in his way.

And then Chief Magistrate Jabiru caught sight of Kokako.

"Him!" he screeched. "Kokako the sweeper! He destroyed the *Oyon*! He was working for the other cities all along!"

"Leave him alone!" Anna roared, running up then, panting a bit in the heat. I made myself visible to the lot of them and leapt in front of Kokako as a few confused guards closed in. Anna joined me, guarding Kokako's back, as the magistrates of the other cities, with some of their officers and the patrol that had tried to arrest us, hurried up. I noticed that they had paused to tie olive branches to their spears, as their own sign of truce.

"A sand-goblin!" a guardsman said. "They're in league with sand-goblins!"

"I'm not a goblin, and I wish you humans would learn to tell one Old Thing from another."

To tell the truth, I was as nervous as the soldiers facing me. Truce or not, I didn't see how we could talk our way out of this, since the cold, stone lump that was Barramundi wasn't real evidence, and we were badly outnumbered. And if they hadn't believed someone as well-known as Annapurna Khanum …

Chief Magistrate Jabiru was telling the story of finding Kokako standing amid the ashy ruins of the altar, his voice getting more and more shrill and excited. He shook his fist at Kokako and announced, "You see, there he is, bold as brass, expecting us to believe his tale of rock-folk and sand-goblins," as if the boy's presence in front of them all was somehow proof of what he'd done.

"Nonsense," said Annapurna Khanum briskly. "Really, how can you know so little about your own land? Kokako, tell these gentlemen and ladies about Lord Barramundi."

So he did. When he got to the bits that happened after we left Annapurna Khanum, I noticed she pulled out her notebook and started scribbling. Anna met my gaze and rolled her eyes. I also noticed that neither Annapurna Khanum nor Kokako mentioned that Lord Barramundi was related to the famous explorer. That sort of thing would probably just distract Magistrate Jabiru and convince him we were all in league.

All the time Kokako was talking, Chief Magistrate Jabiru kept muttering under his breath, getting puffier and puffier with indignation. "Stuff and nonsense!" he burst out, when Kokako, with a deep sigh, said, "… and then we came back."

"You seriously expect us to believe that some old sack with a rock in it is a sorcerer?" The chief magistrate kicked the blanket of utter night, yelped, and tried to hop on one foot. His chins wobbled and he teetered, a bit like the siege tower had. He didn't fall, but only because the commander of the Keastipol city watch took him firmly by the elbow and pulled him upright again.

The commander prodded the bag with her spear. "Easy enough to test," she said. "Open it and let him out. Thaw him, or whatever it is you do."

"No!" Anna, Kokako, and I all shouted at once.

"It was hard enough getting him in there in the first place," Anna said. "He'd just do his disappearing trick, and go off to cause trouble for someone else."

"Not a good idea," Annapurna Khanum agreed. "Not without another sorcerer here to deal with him."

That started the magistrates arguing with one another. Apparently there weren't very many sorcerers at all in the Great Southern Continent. They thought there might be a woman up in Mundiwindipol, which wasn't too far away, but she was terribly old and didn't like to travel, and there was that man in Yannitharrapol, but that was very, very far away, and the girl who lived in Mikatarrapol had gone off to Whenualand to study, and even if they sent for her, she was too young and probably couldn't stand up to a sorcerer like Barramundi, except of course there wasn't really a sorcerer in the sack and it was all a trick …

When the soldiers from the various cities started getting into it, shouting at one another about what should be done, with their hands on their weapons, I decided we had a problem.

I tugged at Kokako, getting him to bend down so I could whisper in his ear. "The Wind Dancers—just now, back on the hill, they said to tell you that you can call the Firebird if you need her. Because you're her friend, she said. Maybe you should."

Kokako looked at me and bit his lip. "But I don't want her to burn people," he protested. His voice was shaking a bit. "I don't want to be thrown in the harbor, I don't want people to start killing one another, but I don't want to burn people up, either, trying to stop them."

"Don't think like these idiots," I said. "You must know the Firebird better than that. Did she seem to you like a creature who goes around burning people?"

"No. She just sings. Even when she speaks, her voice gets

inside you and makes you see the world—makes the world brighter. More real."

"Well, then," I said. "Call her, Kokako. She won't come if you don't—she can't." I was fairly certain that was true. Some magics work that way. You have to ask. "You need to invite her!" I told him.

"Firebird?" Kokako called faintly, looking around as if he expected to see her hiding among the soldiers. And then a bit louder. "Firebird! Firebird, um, if you're not too busy—help?"

The Firebird must have had her own way of traveling that was not very different from Lord Barramundi's. I'll swear she was nowhere near us. And then, she was. A streak of fire divided the sky and swooped over the encampment with a sound like water on a hot frying pan. Soldiers shouted and flung themselves to the ground. Chief Magistrate Jabiru dove to the ground as well, hiding behind the watch commander, who was still on her feet, shading her eyes and staring into the sky.

"Tell them about her," Anna said. "Tell them all! Flytch! Banksy! Everyone has to be able to see Kokako!"

The two big pirates heaved Kokako up, holding him by his feet and ankles, so he was more or less standing in the air at pirate shoulder height, wobbling a bit and looking very nervous. "*Quiet!*" Anna bellowed, cupping her hands around her mouth, and "Quiet!" roared Banksy and Mister Flytch.

"Listen! Kokako needs to tell you *all* something." Anna stressed "all" because only the magistrates and their guards had heard, before.

The shouting and pointing and jabbering stopped, and the

soldiers and magistrates looked away from the fiery streak in the sky, back to Kokako. The people of Keastipol crowded the city battlements, silent and straining to hear.

"Don't bother about Barramundi," I said quietly, looking up at him. "It's the Firebird that's important now."

Kokako took a deep breath.

"We've all made a terrible mistake," he began. "Tero Korax the Wanderer never meant for us to keep the *Oyon* locked up like some sort of antique. It was an egg, the Firebird's egg. You're fighting over *nothing*. The *Oyon* wasn't destroyed. It hatched, the way it should have a hundred years ago! Listen to her, the way our ancestors should have done!"

He looked around. Everyone was looking at him, all the magistrates, all the soldiers, all the people on the wall.

"Um," said Kokako. He wobbled, and Mister Flytch and Banksy steadied him. "Um, that's all, I guess. And it wasn't my fault, there *was* a sorcerer, like Annapurna Khanum told you. He kidnapped the Firebird. I rescued her. So there."

I stopped paying any attention to Kokako, and so did everyone else. The Firebird was circling slowly over the camp and the city now. She looked larger than she had before, twice, no, three times the size of an eagle. Sparks dripped off her trailing plumes and floated gently down like snowflakes, like drifting petals, vanishing just before they touched any of the upturned faces or the tinder-dry ground. She came down lower and lower, until she hovered over Kokako, her wings spread as though she would wrap them around him. The air around her was hot, like it is when you open an oven door, but it didn't burn us. She dipped her head to Kokako's upturned face. She said something, but he never told even me what it was. Then she soared up and over the camp once more, and perched on the arch above the city gate.

And the Firebird sang.

CHAPTER FOURTEEN

# In which the Firebird sings

I don't know how to describe the Firebird's song. Even words can't truly make you feel what we all felt, listening to her that day.

I could tell you that her music was like, oh, rich, warm wooden flutes and sweet silver whistles and deep solemn bag-pipes. It painted pictures in the minds of everyone who heard it. We saw the land, the whole of the Great Southern Continent. We felt, in our blood and bones, the stretching height of the forests, the green secret shadows of the ferny jungles, the mist-pale mountains rising into cool, stone-scented air, the whisper of the bleached gold grass, the strength and freedom and the awesome vastness of the red deserts … the scattered farms, the villages, the seventy cities, where people had made a hundred years of peace. That was what the song showed people how to see, the quiet, calm, and yet exciting joy of the land, that was all one land, all one people, no matter what color they chose to call the sky.

I could tell you, too, that it made us remember, each and every one of us, people that we had lost. It reminded us of forests and fields turned to barren wastelands of stumps and sticks and bones and broken blades, of stone walls fallen and gray rain drumming on deserted streets.

You remember that I told you the seventy cities of the Great Southern Continent used to go to war all the time, not even over big questions, but over trivial little things—was blue or azure the best word to describe the sky, was Nukiwarrapol or Mooloogoolipol the first city to invent the telescope—*stupid* things, as though truth could be discovered through destruction and blood and death. Sometimes you have to choose to fight, when a crocodile is about to eat someone or a dragon is ravaging your land, but the Firebird's song reminded people that the need had to be great, that pride and greed were stupid reasons to destroy life and beauty, and that almost always, there was a better way. The land, of which the Firebird was the heart, wanted peace. And the song sang deep into their blood and bones, and showed them why.

Well, that was how it seemed to me, anyway. No one who heard the Firebird's song could ever hold life and their land so lightly again.

"She's going to go and sing over all the other cities, too," Kokako said softly, though I think only I heard him.

The Firebird gave one last, chiming chord of laughter, like fire and the light of jewels, and soared into the sky again.

Everyone was very quiet.

"Well," said one of the magistrates. Just that. "Well." He wiped his eyes.

ରରରରର

And then, finally, there was time to greet all our friends properly, as all the crowd around us broke up into murmuring clusters of people. Mister Flytch and Banksy set Kokako back on the ground. Mister Flytch picked Anna up and swung her around, which was a bit dangerous, as she still had a sword in her hand.

"I take it you got my note," Anna said, when her feet were firmly planted again.

Mister Flytch laughed. "Yes, well, I got it. I don't have a clue what it says, though. It's a good thing your mother can read your handwriting."

"It was perfectly clear, Flytch. Maybe you should think about getting eyeglasses."

"The problem is *not* with my eyes, Captain."

"Captain, dear! And Torrie! And young Kokako! Not eaten by monsters, after all! Old Flytch was getting a bit worried." Mirimick ruffled up my fur and gave Kokako a hug.

"The seams are all tight," and, "We're ready to sail when you give the word, Captain," reported Banksy and Galeata.

Anna was saying something about buying pots to plant her seeds in, when, "You're back!" screamed a girl's voice that sounded too young to be any of the women pirates, and a girl with red flowers stuck in her hair flung herself at Kokako,

knocking Jix right off his head as she hugged him almost as hard as Flytch had hugged Anna.

"*Gak!*" said Kokako. "Um, hi, Delena. Um, Anna, Torrie, this is Delena. She sweeps the spiders out of the *Oyon*-Shrine."

"Nice to meet you," Anna said, with a wicked grin. "We've heard so much about you."

"Really?" Delena looked sideways at Kokako and blushed.

I looked around for the bundle of the blanket of utter night. It had been right here when Chief Magistrate Jabiru kicked it …

Anna's mother caught my eye and gave a little jerk of her chin away from all the humans. She rose gracefully to her feet—this time she was dressed in the fashion of Callipepla, with baggy silk trousers caught in tight at the ankle, and a wide-sleeved caftan down to her knees, with a long brocade vest over it, although her turban was still very untidy and her hair still stuck out beneath it in spikes. One of her wide sleeves sagged in a very inelegant and heavy way.

"I think it's probably best if I take my Wicked Uncle, Torrie," Annapurna Khanum said.

I peeked into her sleeve, and yes, it was the blanket of utter night and Barramundi she had tucked in there.

"I was going to ask you to do that," I admitted, with a sigh of relief. "If we leave him here, he's bound to get out and cause more trouble." If there was a sorcerer who could deal with Barramundi, it was his older sister, Anna's grandmother. Who was sort of a friend of mine, in case I haven't mentioned that before.

"Hey," said Anna softly, joining us. "What happened to Barramundi, Torrie? You didn't let the magistrates have him?"

Annapurna Khanum patted her sleeve. "We're scheming and plotting," she said. "I'm going to take him to your grandmother, as soon as I find a ship heading north. Then I'll wait for your father to come home to Erythroth."

"Oh," said Anna. "I … um, well, I thought you could come with me. On *Shrike*."

Annapurna Khanum suddenly kissed her daughter's cheek. "I know, dear. But you're sailing to the Granite Isles to take your Prince Frederik his trees, and I … well, you're right, you know. It's been so long—it's time I went home." For just a moment, she looked a little sad, thinking of Anna's father, Captain Icterus of the merchant ship *Oriole*. "I do miss him, you know."

"I know."

"Anyway," said Annapurna, "I've got to write a book about the desert edge, and *Oriole* is as good a place to do it as any, despite what some people say about my handwriting getting worse at sea—it's certainly better than yours is on land, Anna."

Anna snorted, and her mother grinned.

"Icterus and I will sail to the Granite Isles sometime soon. With any luck, we'll catch you in port. Maybe we'll even bring your grandmother."

"Are you coming back to Keastipol any time?" Kokako asked wistfully, escaping the curious magistrates to join us, with Delena tagging after him. "I thought maybe, um, well, you might like to explore the deserts some more. Or something."

"Of course I'm coming back," said Annapurna Khanum, and her eyes gleamed. "All that space, that sky ... the red horizons ... you know, no one's ever crossed the deserts from east to west, Kokako."

"I know," Kokako said, and his eyes gleamed, too.

Annapurna Khanum looked thoughtful. "It won't be easy," she said.

"Of course not."

"I've never had an apprentice before."

Kokako, slowly, started to grin. "I've never been an apprentice before," he said.

"It's a deal," Annapurna Khanum said, and offered him her hand, the one that didn't have Barramundi up its sleeve.

We drifted back into the crowd of people, and it was merely a crowd of people now, not an army. Annapurna was alternately asking Anna about how she'd rescued Captain Icterus from the pirate-queen, and explaining to Kokako that she was going to enrol him at the Academy at once, so he could start studying, to be ready for when she came back. It seemed to me he even looked taller, a young tree stretching up into the sun—all his dreams, the life of a scientist that he'd hoped to have, were within his reach again.

"Parliament had better meet to decide what to do with the *Oyon*-Shrine, now that we don't need it for the *Oyon*," a magistrate was saying, as we wandered past.

"A library."

"A museum."

"The Academy needs more space for its classes."

"We need to elect a new magistrate first," said one of the city councillors from Keastipol. "Chief Magistrate Jabiru hasn't behaved at all the way a magistrate should. Accusing the boy without any proof. Stirring up a mob. Not magisterial behavior at all."

Nobody mentioned that half the city had been quite happy to join the mob, without asking any questions about the truth at all. That's humans for you.

But so was this: the people of Keastipol wandered into the camp, and the soldiers wandered into the city. People greeted old friends, and tried to sell one another kebabs and pastries and candied lemon-peel. In almost no time the camp started to look like a market.

"Maybe it's time to eat," I suggested hopefully.

Delena the spider-girl gave me a wide-eyed look. "Does your pet sand-goblin bite?" she asked Kokako behind her hand.

"I'm *not* a goblin. I'm——"

"No," said Kokako loudly. "At least, not very often."

We all headed into the city. Anna sent some of the pirates off to buy meat and spices and vegetables and sticky pastries, so we could have a feast on *Shrike*, to celebrate our return. They also, very sensibly, bought flowerpots for all the seeds we had collected.

And, that, in the end, was about it. A few days later, it was time to leave. Annapurna Khanum, with the blanket of utter night and Lord Barramundi safely hidden at the bottom of her pack, had already sailed on a ship heading north to Erythroth, to find her husband and his ship. We said our farewells to Kokako and the Great Southern Continent, and Anna and I and the crew of the *Shrike* set sail for the Granite Isles, with the roof of our aftercastle covered in pots of sprouting trees. (I admit I helped the seeds along, to get them to sprout so quickly——that's the sort of magic we Old Things do quite happily.)

～～～～～

"So," Anna said one evening, as we sat atop the forecastle watching the first stars dipping below the horizon with every wave. "Tell me about my grandmother."

"Your grandmother?" I asked, gathering up my thoughts. I'd been thinking that I was feeling a bit homesick, actually. Anna and *Shrike*'s crew were going to make the Granite Isles

their home port, but it wasn't my home. In the end, it's good to go home, to rest for a while between adventures. In time, I knew that my feet would grow itchy for wandering again, and I would be off on another adventure. But just then, thinking of Annapurna Khanum sailing north, I longed for the scent of cold water and pine needles, the sight of carpets of white trilliums beneath the ash and maple trees, the songs of robins and red-winged blackbirds, and most of all, my own cosy den on *my* hilltop, beneath the roots of an oak five centuries old. I wasn't really listening to what Anna had said.

She poked me in the ribs. "Wake up. You know, my grandmother, who I didn't even know was a sorcerer? Lord Barramundi's older sister? She's a friend of yours, and you never told me."

"Well, I didn't know she was your grandmother," I said. I stretched, thinking of the adventures I'd had, that had gotten mixed up with Anna's grandmother. And because I was feeling a bit homesick, I thought of the first time I'd ever run into her, an adventure that had happened partly in my own Wild Forest.

"Ah," I said, and I grinned happily. "What you want is the story about my friend Wren, who went off to rescue a prince who'd been turned into a snake. And how she and I got mixed up with a mysterious, not-quite-human wandering minstrel named Rookfeather."

Anna's father and mother were bound to sail to the Granite Isles to see their daughter again before too long, and with them, I could sail home to the north. No need to feel homesick. Home was always there, waiting for me. And meanwhile, there was nothing like a good story to pass the time.

I climbed up and found a comfortable perch on the rail, raising my voice so that the sailors lazing around on deck, and even Mister Flytch at the tiller in the aftercastle, could hear me.

"It all began one spring long ago, when I went up to High Morroway in the mountains, looking for an adventure ..."

The natural history of the Great Southern Continent visited by Torrie and Anna is fairly obviously based on that of Australia. Many thanks (and a city) go to Allen Keast, not only for his lifelong friendship and inspiration, but for his book, *Australia and the Pacific Islands: A Natural History* (Random House, 1966), which was almost as good as an expedition of exploration for me, without the danger of crocodiles and getting lost in the desert. If I have plants flowering or bearing ripe seeds at the wrong time of year, or growing in not quite the right climate, it's not his fault; I did my best, but Anna needed those seeds for Prince Frederik's new forests. Allen Keast is also responsible for Annapurna; after reading *Pirate-Queen*, he wrote me a letter that revealed the secret history of Annapurna's childhood. When the letter arrived, Annapurna became Annapurna Khanum, jumping right into the story at the point I was working on, to the great surprise of Anna and myself. (Torrie probably expected something like that to happen all along.)

Of course, the Great Southern Continent isn't meant to be exactly like the real Australia; it's just inspired by parts of it in landscape, plants, and animals. Although I borrowed many place names from Australia, the pronunciation guides in the glossary are my own, and aren't necessarily how you should say "Mundaring" or "Bookabee" if you actually go to Australia. The culture of the human inhabitants, on the other hand, has no connection to Australia at all. (You might recognize the *Oyon*-Shrine if you look at pictures of Athens …) The Old Things are as much my own as the northern Old Things of Torrie's Wild Forest; that is, they're partly inspired by creatures from traditional folklore and mythology, and partly made up. I took Kokako's name from that of a bird that is neither Australian nor Greek; the kokako is a New Zealand bird with the scientific name of *Callaeas cinerea*. Like many New Zealand birds, it's endangered. (And whenua, which I've incorporated into the name Whenualand, where Kokako's father came from, is a Maori word for the land.)

In case you missed the first
Torrie adventure, be sure to read

By **K.V Johansen**

**Illustrated by**
**Christine Delezenne**

Torrie, the Old Thing from the Wild Forest, helps Anna and
her ragtag crew of retired pirates on a dramatic quest to
rescue Anna's captive father.

## About the author & illustrator

K.V. Johansen is the author of six novels for young people
and a series of picture books. She lives in Sackville, New
Brunswick.

Christine Delezenne is the illustrator of several books
for young people. She lives in Montreal.